The ASSASSIN

Liam O'Flaherty titles published by Wolfhound Press:

The Pedlar's Revenge and Other Stories (1976)
All Things Come of Age: A Rabbit Story (1977) – for children
The Test of Courage (1977) – for children
The Ecstacy of Angus (1978) – a novella
Famine (1979) – a novel
The Black Soul (1981) – a novel
Shame the Devil (1981) – autobiography
Short Stories by Liam O'Flaherty (1982)
The Wilderness (1978, 1986) – a novel
Skerrett (1977, 1988) – a novel
Insurrection (1988) – a novel

Limited first editions, handbound, signed and numbered

The Pedlar's Revenge and Other Stories (1976)
The Wilderness (1978)

The ASSASSIN

Liam O'Flaherty

WOLFHOUND PRESS

This edition 1988
WOLFHOUND PRESS
68 Mountjoy Square,
Dublin 1.

© 1988, 1983, 1928 Liam O'Flaherty

First edition: London 1928
First published by Wolfhound Press 1983

British Library Cataloguing in Publication Data

O'Flaherty, Liam
    The assassin.
    I Title
    823'.914   [F]   PR6029.F5

    ISBN 0-86327-006-9

Cover design: Jan de Fouw
Typesetting: Redsetter Ltd., Dublin.
Printed by the Guernsey Press Co. Ltd., Guernsey.

THE ASSASSIN

TO
MY CREDITORS

CHAPTER ONE

AT three o'clock in the afternoon, Michael McDara alighted from a tram-car at the corner of Findlater's Church. He crossed the road and moved northwards until he came to the corner of Hardwicke Street. He halted there and looked around him cautiously. First, he looked down the street by which he had come. Then he looked northwards towards the corner of Dorset Street. Finally, he looked up Hardwicke Street. Then, having made a complete and careful examination of his surroundings, he set off up Hardwicke Street. But he had not gone three paces when he halted suddenly and returned to the corner. He looked around again in all directions, as if waiting for somebody.

'Blazes!' he said to himself. 'This won't do. Any fool could spot something by the way I'm carrying on. What's the matter with me? Nobody knows anything yet. Eh?'

He was trembling with excitement. He noticed this and took his hands out of the pockets of his shabby raincoat. He cupped his hands in front of his mouth, blew into his palms and then rubbed them together violently. If anybody were really watching, it would appear that he was trembling with the cold.

He was a young man of medium size, very slightly built, with a marked stoop in his slender shoulders. His cheeks were pale and thin, with deep, vertical lines. His hands looked delicate and thin. They were covered, on the back, with blue veins. His blue eyes were sunk slightly. They had a harassed look. But they were also cold and subtle. They looked intent and almost fierce, as if guarding some secret. His thin lips were drawn close over his mouth. His tall forehead was deadly white.

His clothes were shabby. A long whitish raincoat was buttoned about his throat and reached half-way down his calves. It was very loose and floppy, with uneven rim, as if it didn't belong to him, but was borrowed from somebody stouter than himself. It hung like a shroud about him. One or two of the buttons were missing and the pocket on the left side was ripped at the seam. He wore a tweed cap, perched jauntily on the side of his head, with the peak down far over his left eye. A bunch of scraggy fair hair protruded from the upside of the cap. The legs of his blue trousers, showing beneath the rim of the raincoat, were shabby and wrinkled, as if they had gone through a fumigator. His boots were the only respectable things on his body. They were of a good make and well polished.

His appearance was that of a grocer's curate out of work. Or else, one of those shabby fellows, with a sour expression and a hang-dog mouth, that haunt betting shops of an afternoon, brooding over fantastic schemes for making a vast fortune.

He moved away again up Hardwicke Street. He walked slowly, examining the houses on either side

8

of the street. That gloomy street looked more desolate than usual. It was a March day. The air was
bitterly cold. There had been intermittent rain and
frost for the past two days. Now the cobbled roadway was covered with a thick loam, that sent up a
faint smoke and a smell of dried offal. Here and
there pools of water lay between holes in the cobble-
stones. The gaunt houses, some of them hundreds
of years old, seemed to stand out, when he looked
at them, like ghouls, dirty, bedraggled, ashamed of
their existence. There were arches and courtyards,
used in another age, when the street was a fashionable quarter, and each house had stables and a
retinue of menials attached to it. Now these arches
and courtyards looked like unused caves. The whole
street was strangely silent, like a tomb; or rather
like the cloister of a monastery. A man, no matter
how drunk, would think twice before uttering a loud
shout in the place. Although it bordered on a main
thoroughfare, it seemed as remote as a mountain top.

McDara became more and more pleased with the
look of the street as he advanced. He thought:

'This is the goods. A fellow can just slip in here
and slip out again as easy as clockwork. I think I'll
pitch here.'

However, he had almost reached the far end of
the street before he saw a sign in a window. He
started when he saw the sign and again his excitement returned. Here, so to speak, was the first
scene in his drama. The first contact filled him with

9

terror. He had to reason with himself, in order to calm his nerves. And while he reasoned with himself, he walked across the street towards the house, where he had seen the sign ROOM TO LET in a window.

It was a house slightly cleaner than the rest, with a red door. There were two geranium pots in the ground-floor windows. That attracted him, because a landlady who is careful of her house in such a quarter is generally a respectable woman and not likely to be a drunkard or one that is fond of gossiping to the police about her lodgers. He walked up to the door and knocked loudly. Then, as he waited, he began to tremble again. When he heard steps approaching in the hall, he wanted to run away. He had to bite his lips, one after the other, in order to prevent himself from taking to flight. Then the door opened and a small, fat servant, with a stupid face, appeared, scratching the back of her head. She eyed him with open mouth.

'I'm looking for a room,' he said.

'Wha'?' she said stupidly. 'A room?'

'Yes,' he thought. 'That's good. She's a fool.'

'Yes,' he said aloud. 'I see there's a room to let here and . . .'

'Wait a minute,' she interrupted. 'I'll go an' see. Will ye come into the hall?'

He stepped into the hall. She closed the door and went off to get the landlady. He looked about him suspiciously. There was a faint smell in the hall, a smell of old age. It was clean, dusted and swept, but still that smell remained, like the smell in an old tomb. Opposite the hallstand there was a big picture. When he saw the picture he started. It was the charge at Balaclava.

'God!' he said. 'A soldier's wife. I better make a bunk.'

A horrible suspicion entered his mind, a suspicion that he had walked plump into the house of a detective belonging to the secret police.

'But that's ridiculous,' he said to himself savagely. 'How could anybody know anything yet? Don't be a fool.'

A deep bass voice made him start. He looked towards the end of the hall and saw a stout woman approach. He took off his cap and was on the point of making a slight bow, when he jerked himself erect and clicked his heels like a soldier.

'I'm looking for a room,' he said politely.

'I see,' said the landlady, in a suspicious voice.

Then she approached until she stood beside him, with her arms folded on her bosom.

She was a heavy woman, about forty, with prominent busts, red cheeks and dark eyes. The lower part of her face resembled the face of a lioness. McDara did not like the look of her at first. He saw that she was suspicious of him.

'I'll make some excuse,' he thought, 'and clear out.'

'How long would ye want it for?' she said severely.

'Well,' he said, changing from one foot to another and coughing, 'I don't know exactly. Maybe three months, let us say. Ye see, I was thinking of . . .'

Suddenly an idea entered his head. He said to himself:

'Silly. She'd be the best sort after all.'

'You see,' he said aloud, 'I've just come over from Liverpool. I'm looking for a job.'

'Oh! Well,' she said roughly, 'I can't keep lodgers that can't pay their rent.'

'You needn't worry about that,' he said, 'I have a pension. But what I was thinking about was this. . . .'

He paused and looked up at her boldly.

'There's a certain hostility in this city to ex-soldiers. I want to tell you that I'm an ex-soldier, so that . . . if you have any objection on that score . . .'

The landlady uttered an exclamation and shrugged her shoulders.

'Indeed,' she said, with an angry gesture, 'and why should I? My husband was killed on the Somme. A sergeant in the Dublin Fusiliers. I'd like to hear any strap that 'ud have anything to say against an ex-soldier. But . . .'

Her voice changed again and became cold.

'Still,' she said, 'I'm a poor woman and I've been let down many a time. . . .'

'Oh! Well,' said McDara, 'as far as that goes, I have a full pension. I was discharged for total disablement. If I take the room I'll pay you by the month in advance.'

'I see,' she said.

She became more friendly.

'Would ye care to have a look at the room?' she said.

He followed her upstairs to the second floor. She entered a large room, facing the street. It was spotlessly clean, and although the furniture was of a humble sort, the room had a comfortable, homely appearance. There was a large open grate, a gas-cooker, a sink with water laid on and a little cup-board with kitchen ware and cooking utensils. In the centre of the room there was a large deal table, with an oilcloth over the end of it.

'If ye like,' she said, 'ye could do yer own cooking, or else we could give ye breakfast. We don't give dinners except on Sunday.'

'This would be just the thing,' thought McDara; 'completely cut off.'

'I like the room,' he said. 'I'd prefer to do my own cooking. Just a servant to clean up in the morning and make the bed. That's all I'd want. How much is it?'

'Well,' she said. 'Let me see. It's fourteen shil-lings a week. But considering yer a . . . Have ye got yer army papers?'

McDara started, and then he said hurriedly:

'Oh! Yes, of course. Here they are.'

He put his hand inside his raincoat and fumbled

13

about for a long time, opening a number of buttons. Then he pulled out a packet of papers.

There was a discharge paper in the name of John Henry Carter, discharged without a mark of any sort against him, for disablement incurred while on active service. He showed her this and another paper, also purporting to belong to John Henry Carter, a seaman in the British Mercantile Marine, with discharges from various ships, on which John Henry Carter had served as an able seaman. A third paper he held in his hand, and when she had inspected the first two, he said, opening the third one:

'This is my passport. I've been around a lot since I left the army. I had a job in Mexico for a while, with an oil company.'

The passport requested all and sundry to give every assistance to the British subject known as John Henry Carter, in the name of the British Crown.

The landlady was very much impressed by these papers. McDara put them back within his clothes and said, with sudden fervour:

'It's damned hard, you know, when you return to your own country, after spending years in the trenches fighting for freedom, then knocked about the world, trying to save a few pounds, to come back here and be afraid to show your face, for fear people would laugh at you, or maybe spit at you, for having made a fool of yourself. I'm broken in health. I had to give up the sea. Now I suppose I'll have to take up a job as an insurance agent or a traveller in something. And I had a good education.'

'Ah!' said the landlady. 'Every one has his own troubles. Well . . . Considering yer an ex-soldier, we'll say ten-and-sixpence, including gas. I think that's fair.'

'Very well,' said McDara. 'I'll pay you right now a month in advance.'

He took out a note-case and opened it in front of her, to show her that it was well filled. He gave her a five-pound note.

'Ye can give me the change,' he said, 'when I come back with my kit. I left my bags at a hotel.'

Two hours later he arrived at the house with two suitcases. The fat servant again admitted him. He brought his suitcases to his room and locked the door. He was perspiring. Then he stood in the middle of the floor, stretched his arms above his head and drew in a deep breath. He dropped his arms to his side and thought:

'Now the fun begins. Slow. Slow. I must go very slow. Watch every move.'

His face lit up with a strange frenzy. His sunken eyes became exalted. His lips opened and he stood for several seconds, staring vacantly at the wall, as if looking at a vision. Then he shrugged himself again and took off his raincoat. He took up the smaller of his suitcases, put it on the table and opened it. It was packed with old clothes, similar in kind to the clothes on his body. There were odds and ends, articles of toilet and the knick-knacks that a wandering man picks up in his travels. He was about to unpack this case, when he started and a look of terror came into his eyes. He rushed to the door and saw that it was securely locked. Then he rushed back to the large suitcase that was still on the floor. He unlocked it hurriedly, opened it and examined its contents. It contained a new and fashionable suit of light brown clothes, a light brown overcoat, also fashionably made and of good material, a hat, a shirt, socks, shoes, a collar, a tie and a coloured handkerchief, of the kind that is worn as an ornament on the outside breast pocket.

He nodded, closed the suitcase and locked it again. Then he unbuttoned his coat, waistcoat and trousers. He took a linen band from about his waist and laid it out on the table. From various pockets in this belt he took little bundles of five-pound notes. He counted them carefully. There was a sum of four hundred and fifty pounds in all. He put the money back again into the belt and put the belt around his waist.

'That's right,' he thought. 'Four fifty. I have forty-five in my note-case. Let us say two hundred for the job. That leaves two fifty afterwards. The forty-five for current expenses should carry me over until it's done. Good.'

He arranged his dress and unlocked the door.

'If she came with the change,' he thought, 'and found the door locked, she might suspect something.

Everything must be as casual as possible. It's the tiniest mistake that spoils everything.'

He settled the room to his satisfaction and then went out to purchase food. On his way out the land-lady handed him the change and a key.

'Good,' he thought, as he went down the street towards a dairy shop at the corner, 'she has perfect confidence in me. I'll make love to her too. Where did I read that? They say it always pays to . . . if it's done in a certain way.'

He returned to his room at six o'clock, with food and a bundle of newspapers. He studied these news-papers until far into the night.

CHAPTER TWO

AT nine o'clock next morning McDara left the house. It was very cold. There was a glaze of frost on the ground. The sky was clear. Everything looked bright, sharp and fierce. The intense energy of a frosty day in spring was in the atmosphere.

He moved along hurriedly, with intent gaze, breathing deep draughts of the fierce air, that seemed to have been provided for him specially by nature, to steel his heart against fear, on that day when he was about to set his plot in motion.

He moved away with stooping shoulders, enveloped in his shabby, whitish raincoat as in a shroud, dragging his feet like a peasant. His eyes glittered. He kept looking about him furtively, although he made repeated efforts to walk casually, just like an out-of-work peasant come to town in search of employment. But no matter how much he tried to be calm and casual, the secret in his mind irritated him so much that he kept listening to every sound and glancing furtively at everybody that passed.

He boarded a tram-car at Findlater's Church and went to Nelson Pillar. There he dismounted and crossed over to the corner of Talbot Street, opposite Burton's. He stood there, with his hands in his pockets. He had no reason for standing there, and indeed, for a man seeking privacy in his movements, it is the worst corner in Dublin to stand at. As it is crowded at all hours, detectives find it a favourite place for observing their prey. But even though he knew this, and perhaps because he knew it, he could not resist the temptation to stand there with his hands in his pockets, looking about him.

This spot, so dear to every Dubliner, had a curious attraction for him, and further, he felt disinclined to begin on the work he had in hand. So he stood there watching the people, listening to the medley of sound, inhaling the strange smells through his nostrils. Newsboys shouting their wares, women with shawls arguing with one another and with two policemen who were ordering them away from the base of Nelson's monument, the rattle of tram-cars, the continual shuffle of feet passing and repassing, ragged people, well-dressed people, the smell of oranges, the smell of beer passing on drays, the hooting of motor-cars and the loud cries of street arabs, all came to his eyes, ears and nose, entered his mind and filled him with an intoxicated consciousness of the romance of his intended act.

He had been standing there about five minutes, as if in a trance, when a burly fellow of great stature, wearing a thick black overcoat and a wide black hat, suddenly appeared beside him. He looked up, feeling the big man's presence, and saw a pair of little cunning eyes peeping from beneath the wide rim of the black hat. A detective! The big fellow looked for a moment only, but his little cunning eyes

19

seemed in that moment to have probed down into the inmost caverns of McDara's soul. There was a smell from the man too, a warm, heavy, animal smell, as from some monster of the forest, that is merciless in its brutality. So McDara thought as he stood beside the burly man, shivering like an aspen.

Then he smiled and thought: 'Let him look. I defy him to see into my mind.' And then the big man moved away, shoving his way casually through the people, moving his enormous feet sideways, silently, like a great phantom. The listening ear, the shrewd, inquisitive eye, the huge muscle of authority!

McDara spat into the roadway, wiped his mouth on his sleeve and then moved off, with one shoulder raised slightly and his hands deep in his shabby pockets. If the big fellow looked back after him, he would notice nothing. The thug! Now McDara felt exhilarated. He felt inclined to lead that fool of a policeman a nice dance around town, by exciting his suspicions. But suddenly he thought that apart from the project in his mind, which was yet secure, there were former acts against him, which only his concealed identity prevented them from . . .

He rushed across the road in front of a tram and ran to the corner of Mary Street. There he broke into a sharp walk. He kept saying to himself, clenching his teeth:

'Have I no more guts than this? Why am I acting the goat?'

He had got to the end of Mary Street when he halted again and thought:

'Perhaps I had better take a look around first before seeing him. What? I can't be too careful.'

This thought, that he was acting without proper caution, so disconcerted him, that he felt weak at the knees and wanted to go back to his lodgings. He had to make a great effort before he could persuade himself to move on. He entered Capel Street and turned northwards. Now he was in the heart of a slum district. The smells, of which his senses were peculiarly conscious, became more violent and nauseous. But to him they were as sweet and intoxicating as they were unpleasant to the normal citizen. They whetted his appetite for the act he was going to perform. Everything here excited a savage hatred of society in him: barefooted children with a hectic flush on their pale, starved faces, tottering old people with all manner of disease scarring their wasted features, offal in the streets, houses without doors and with broken windows, a horrifying and monotonous spectacle of degrading poverty and misery everywhere. The fœtid air reeked with disease.

He came to a little huckster's shop at the corner of a lane. Over the door was the name Mary McFetterich.

'This is it,' he said to himself.

He stood opposite it, on the other side of the street, for a minute or so, trying to make up his mind to enter. Again a fit of trembling possessed him and all sorts of fears and suspicions crowded into his mind. Again he had to make a great effort to conquer this palsy. He crossed the street quickly and entered the shop. It was a tiny place, almost filled by a counter, on which there were innumerable articles of all sorts for sale: newspapers, jars of sweets, thread, snuff, loaves of bread, clay pipes and small religious pictures. There was nobody in the shop. But after a few moments he saw an old woman peering through a little door at the far end, through a white curtain. The old woman opened the door and came forward, muttering to herself.

'Frosty mornin',' she said, rubbing her wrinkled hands on her bosom.

She was very thin and she had rheumy eyes. Her nose was hooked. She had a little shawl around her head like a peasant woman.

'Is yer son in?' said McDara. 'You're Mrs. Fetterich, aren't you?'

'Aye,' she said, looking at him cautiously. 'I am. Me son, did ye say? D'ye mean Dan?'

'Yes, Dan,' said McDara. 'I'm a friend of his. I met him in Liverpool. He told me to look him up when I came over here.'

'Aye,' said the old woman, rubbing her wrinkled hands back and forth on the counter. 'In Liverpool, did ye say? Ha! Dan is it ye want to see? A friend of his are ye?'

'Yes,' said McDara, 'I thought I'd prowl in and see him.'

'Yer out early,' said the old woman, still rubbing her hands back and forth along the counter.

McDara suddenly got suspicious of the old woman and felt that he had done a very foolish thing.

'Oh! Well,' he said, 'if he's not in, say I called to see him.'

'Hold on,' she said, suddenly changing her tone. 'Is it Dan ye said?'

'She's mad,' thought McDara.

'Yes, Dan,' he said in a loud voice.

'Oh, then,' she said angrily, 'ye'll not find him in, no matter how early ye come.'

'Ah ha! Has he left here, then?'

'No, he hasn't. But he's not here now.'

'Yes, she is mad,' said McDara to himself. 'She's stark mad.'

'All right. Good morning, Mrs. McFetterich.'

'Hold on now,' she said. 'What's yer hurry? Is it a job ye had for him?'

'Eh?' said McDara.

He paused a moment and then he said:

'Yes. I have a job for him all right.'

The old woman opened her mouth and showed two rows of beautiful yellow teeth. She laughed without making any sound.

'I know ye,' she said, winking a rheumy eye. 'Yer a fine lot of boyos. Go on. Ye'll find him either of three places,' cos he's never here from cock-crow to midnight. The only good habits he has is to get up early and go to bed late. He's gone to the library to read the racin' papers and from there to the back o' Mulligan's to spend the mornin' and from there to Tutty's to back horses all after-noon. It's easy findin' him 'cos he has regular habits. Oh! Aye! I suppose you're another boyo like himself.'

'Thanks very much,' said McDara, raising his cap.

'Good morning to ye,' she said. 'Yer a fine lot o' boyos.'

He dashed out of the shop, anxious to get away from the old woman. He returned to Capel Street and entered the library. It was now nearly half-past ten o'clock and the public reading-room was crowded with men of all ages. Some of them had come in to read, but the majority had entered there because they had nowhere else to go. Here there was a fire and human companionship. Around each news-paper, that was spread on a sort of easel, battened down in the middle by a metal rod, a crowd of dis-reputable characters stood, peering over one another's shoulders. In the middle of the room there was a long table. Periodicals of every description were strewn about this table. Each was in a cover and secured by a clasp. There was a man, young or old, sitting in front of each periodical. Some were read-ing. Others were dozing. Others were watching eagerly, until some coveted periodical should be relinquished by the man that was reading it. They did not seem to care what they read. One man, an old fellow with a boil on his neck, stared without movement of any sort at the picture of an almost nude dancer which lay before him on the page of a society journal. Another old man with a white beard, sitting in front of a copy of a religious journal called *The Irish Rosary*, had taken off his left boot and sock and was paring his toe-nails with a large knife. The old rascal was doing this on purpose to drive away his neighbour who was looking at the naughty pictures in a fashion paper. Nobody noticed him.

McDara walked around the room, examining each group, seeking his friend. He could see him nowhere. A little fellow, in a ragged blue suit, came up and whispered in front of his face:

'Are ye lookin' for anyone, Jack?'

McDara looked at the little fellow angrily. Then a sudden whim seized him.

'Yes,' he said, with a strange smile. 'Do you know him?'

'Who?' said the little fellow, scratching his crutch.

'The Holy Ghost,' said McDara. 'Does he come in here?'

Then he laughed and walked out of the room.

'Hey, lads,' said the little fellow to his companions. 'That fellah is in the rats. Do ye know who he's lookin' for? Holy Smoke, he said.'

Outside the door, McDara stopped a man who was going past with three long poles on a hand-cart.

'Hey, mate,' he said. 'Whereabouts is Mulligan's?'

'Eh?' said the man. 'Mulligan's. Let me see. Ye see that lamp-post there above?'

McDara listened to the directions, thanked the man and walked away. After a few turns he came to a public-house that was painted red and entered the private bar. There in front of him, standing against the counter, with a pint of stout in his hand, was the man he sought.

This man was Daniel McFetterich, commonly known as Gutty Fetch and simply as Gutty among his intimate friends. He was quite tall, but his body was so twisted about, without being in any way deformed, that he looked small. He had very wide shoulders and a head shaped like a triangle. His hair was pitch-black and his face was bronzed a dark brown. He had remarkably thin lips, always clasped together. His cheekbones were very high. The left cheekbone was marked by an old scar, shaped like a half-moon. He also wore a loose raincoat like McDara but of a different colour. His raincoat was dark brown. He wore a check cap. He looked better dressed than McDara. On his remarkably small feet he wore a pair of patent-leather shoes with cloth uppers. He looked like a race-course tout of the better sort.

When McDara entered the bar, Fetch was laughing at something. A small group of men were standing at the counter beside Fetch teasing the barman about his love affairs. One little fat man, wearing a bowler hat, was holding a glass of whisky towards the barman and saying:

'Look at him. He has a face like an angel but he has his little bird and sees her on his half-day off, down by the Dodder banks.'

'Let that pass now,' said the barman in a squeaky voice. 'What are we here for, anyway? Tell me that now. Even the flies have their fun on a clergyman's hat, as a certain prominent citizen once said.'

'Well, you'll never be in his boots, anyway,' said another man.

'Whose boots?' said a fierce-looking man with drooping moustaches.

The group of men gathered around the fierce-looking man and McDara moved up to the far corner of the counter. He beckoned to the barman.

'Sherry,' he said.

Fetch, standing close to McDara, started slightly when he heard McDara's voice. He turned his head, looked at McDara and then put his measure of stout on the counter. McDara nodded casually.

'Cold morning,' he said quietly.

'You said it,' replied Fetch, spitting on the sawdust-covered floor.

He spoke with an American accent.

A ragged little boy appeared at the door and yelled:

'Early Bird. Racing Special.'

'Holy God!' said the man with the hard hat. 'Is it that time?'

'Here you are, sonny,' said the barman to the little boy.

They all eagerly bought the newspapers.

'When did ye land?' whispered Fetch through his teeth.

'Yesterday morning,' said McDara.

The barman brought McDara's sherry. McDara paid and received his change. The crowd of men left the bar, shouting to one another. The fierce-looking man alone remained. He walked around the room, with his hands in the pockets of his overcoat, muttering to himself. The barman retired to the interior of the bar, spread the racing paper and began to study it. McDara and his friend were alone in their corner.

'Well?' said McDara. 'Did you get hold of him yet?'

'Nope,' said Fetch.

'No?' said McDara angrily.

'No,' said Fetch. 'He's not on the horizon. I couldn't do much. Don't want to attract attention. I couldn't get in touch with anybody.'

'Curse it.'

'I've got a map of the location, though.'

'A map?'

'I mean I've nosed around and know every inch of the ground.'

'What good is that? We have to get T.'

'Well, I've only been here a week and I'm takin' no chances. Savvy?'

'Hell!'

'You'll have to work that Judy.'

Suddenly the fierce-looking man, who had been walking around the floor, shouted out to the barman.

'Hey!' he cried. 'Hey, you!'

'What?' said the barman.

The fierce-looking man, instead of replying, looked at the ground and began to search about in his overcoat pockets. His eyebrows protruded like snouts over his little black eyes.

'What's the matter?' said the barman, coming over to the counter.

'What's the matter?' cried the fierce-looking man. 'Russia. Cut their throats. Like this.'

With a long dirty finger he made an imaginary gash across his yellow, wrinkled throat.

'Russia,' he repeated savagely. 'Rips their guts.'

'Who?' said the barman, laughing.

'Who?' said the man. 'The earth and all that's on it.'

'Who so?' said the barman.

'Why so?' yelled the man, suddenly becoming

frenzied with rage. 'Why? Why? Pigs. That's why. Pigs is fallen. Blast an' curse it.'

With that he made a gesture with both hands and dashed out into the street. The barman held his sides and then began to beat the counter with a wet rag.

'God!' he said. 'Can ye beat that?'

'A farmer down the country,' he said to Fetch. 'Lookin' for a tart that robbed him the other night. He's up to-day to the police.'

'Rustled him clean,' said Fetch.

'One hundred and ten quid,' said the barman, returning to his newspaper.

McDara had remained perfectly motionless, without a smile on his face, during this interruption. When the barman went away, he whispered to Fetch:

'It's no use without T. We can't do it on our own.'

Fetch shrugged his shoulders.

'It's up to you,' he said.

'How is that?' said McDara angrily. 'You think you need do nothing only monkey around bars?'

Fetch looked at McDara coldly, licked the side of his mouth with his tongue, winked one eye, spread his legs, put his gloved hands in the pockets of his raincoat and swayed back and forth.

'Nope,' he said. 'How d'ye like my American accent?'

'Come on,' said McDara. 'Let's get out of here.

I'll have to use the girl after all. You'll have to take a message to her.'

Fetch said good morning to the barman and the two men left the public-house.

CHAPTER THREE

A LITTLE after seven o'clock in the evening, three days later, Kitty Mellett knocked at the door of McDara's lodgings. She was admitted by the landlady. She said she wanted to see Mr. Carter. The landlady gave her a chair in the hall and examined her closely, fearing that she might be an improper person. Her appearance was reassuring. She wore glasses and a long raincoat. She carried an umbrella. Her face was neither painted nor powdered. She had a severe thoughtful expression. The landlady decided that it would not be dangerous to admit this person to a gentleman's room.

She went upstairs to McDara's room and presently called down over the banisters telling the visitor to walk up. She pointed out McDara's door which stood ajar. The visitor thanked her, entered the room and closed the door.

McDara was standing in front of the fire with his arms folded. His face gave no sign of recognition as the young woman entered. It seemed from his face that she was a stranger to him. He pointed to a chair without speaking.

The young woman also remained silent. She stood still, with her back to the door, examining McDara's face in wonder. Her eyes moved about over his face and body, as if trying to recognize him. Her eyes gradually became hostile. When he motioned her to a chair, she took off her glasses,

32

folded them and pushed them carelessly into the
pocket of her raincoat. She only wore them as a disguise. Then she advanced a few paces, tossed her
umbrella on to the table and stripped off her raincoat.
She took off her little round cap and began to tidy
her hair. She stood, with widespread feet, in a bold,
masculine attitude.

Without her spectacles and her overcoat she
looked an extremely attractive woman. Her face
was not pretty. It was too strong and masculine and
it lacked care. But she had a magnificent body.
Her hair was pitch-black. She wore it full length,
dressed at the back of her head in plaits and divided
down the middle on the forehead. Her white forehead, with the gleaming, black hair coming down
in a slanting curve on either side, was very beautiful
and exciting. Yet, her cold, grey eyes and her severe
lips belied the promise of amorous charm caused by
her forehead, by her hair, by her long white throat,
by her tapering white hands, by her limbs that were
long and firm, smooth and delicately fashioned, as
if made of marble. Her severe mouth and her cold
grey eyes made her look tantalizing and aggravating;
giving that impression of chastity which leaves so
many beautiful Irish women without husbands; and,
when they do marry, robs their husbands of their
virility. She wore a pretty dark dress that clung to
her figure, showing her beauty proudly; as if to tease
the male with a vision of unattainable charms.

She was thirty, a year younger than McDara.

33

They were old comrades. She had once acted as a sort of aide-de-camp for him, when they were both active in the recent guerrilla wars. She had also been a friend of his at the university. In fact, he had once been in love with her; and it was his romantic, juvenile love for her that first made him a revolutionary.

She sat down by the table and began to rap the board nervously with her fingers.

'Well, Kitty,' said McDara at length. 'Are you glad to see me?'

She looked up at him quickly and said angrily:

'What are you doing here?'

He started. His lips trembled.

'Why?' he said.

'Why?' she answered. 'You know very well why.'

'I don't know of any reason to prevent me from being where I like,' he replied, looking at her intently.

'Don't you?' she said mysteriously. 'I do.'

'What is it?'

'You're a Government spy.'

McDara laughed softly.

'Who told you that?' he said.

She smiled.

'Good Lord!' she said, looking him up and down. 'You're a cool customer. Still! I never knew you even had the guts to be that.'

McDara, instead of becoming angry, continued

34

to laugh. He took a packet of cigarettes from his pocket and proceeded to light one.

'You don't give a damn, I suppose?' she continued.

'No,' he said. 'Not a damn.'

'Well, then,' she said, 'what do you want with me? Who is that funny-looking animal you sent around with a message? Another thug, I suppose?'

'Depends on what you call a thug,' he said. 'He has killed men and I trust he'll kill some more. In that sense of course he is a thug. Who said I was a spy, though? I'd like to know that.'

'Are you sick?' she said. 'I hardly recognize you. Or is this a part of the disguise you have adopted for your spying business? What brought you back to Dublin? Are you going to answer the charges made against you?'

'I'm glad of that,' he said calmly, lighting his cigarette.

'Glad of what?' she said.

'That you don't recognize me.'

'H'm.'

He threw the match into the fire.

'I don't want to be recognized. And as for answering any charges, the more they charge the better I like it.'

'I thought you had changed,' she said vindictively, leaning her elbows on the table and putting her chin in her hands. 'But you haven't changed. You're as vain as ever.'

35

'So.'

'So. You escaped out of jail three years ago. In all probability they let you out by arrangement. You were helped out of the country. And then . . . then you turned traitor. And now you come back here. What have you been doing during the last three years?'

'I've been earning my living.'

'How?'

'Look here, Kitty,' said McDara, coming up to her, 'I didn't ask you to come to ask me questions. You don't know a damn thing about me. So don't be a fool.'

'Don't you dare touch me,' she said.

He stood beside her and looked down on her angry face almost contemptuously.

'I don't want to touch you,' he said harshly. 'I'm not interested in women. I have no time. I was interested in you once. But that's another matter.'

She looked at him hatred.

'You have eyes like a murderer,' she said.

'I might need them for that purpose,' he said softly.

She started. Until now her attitude had been that of a jealous woman. He had escaped from her influence. He had stayed away three years without sending her a letter. He had allowed himself to be accused of being a Government agent without defending himself. And then he had come back, under an assumed name, and treated her as coolly as if his conduct had been unapproachable. Her jealousy was born of that mixture of sex and idealism which is so strange a characteristic of women revolutionaries.

Now, however, as he looked down at her, with his terrible sunken eyes, his muttered words suggested something to her, that robbed her of her jealousy by arousing her curiosity.

'I sent for you,' he said, 'because I have something to discuss with you.'

'What is it?'

'I want you to do something for me.'

She shook her head.

'I'm not going to discuss any secret stunts,' she said, 'with a man who is suspected of being a Government agent.'

He suddenly got angry.

'All right,' he cried. 'Clear out. But keep your mouth shut. Get out of it.'

She laughed.

'Now, Michael,' she said, 'don't lose your temper. Suppose I did go and warn the . . . You know.'

'It's worse being an informer than being suspected of being a Government spy.'

She flushed. He laughed and continued:

'Especially to inform on a man who was once in love with you.'

He suddenly stooped forward, seized her violently by both hands, leaned forward over the table and whispered close to her face:

37

'Kitty. Isn't it funny that now when I have the power in me to make love to you and make you love me, I have no time and I don't want to do it? Isn't that damnable?'

She struggled to free her hands. But he held them tightly.

'Don't move, you fool. You don't know me. I'm not the man you knew. I'm somebody else. You can't play with me. I don't give tuppence about you. I've got something to do and I'm going to use you to help me. I wouldn't if I could help it. But I want to get a man, whom you have to get for me. That's why I sent for you. Now, shut up.'

He suddenly loosed her hands and stood back from the table. His eyes glittered. There was a savage look in his pale face. She jumped to her feet, trembling with fear.

'You beast,' she hissed. 'You're just what you always were, a half-savage. From the wilds of Kerry. Good-bye.'

She began to pick up her coat and cap. Suddenly he rushed to the door, opened it, looked out, closed it again and locked it. He put his back to the door. He thought:

'Now, what have I done? This is damnable.'

They stared at one another.

'What do you mean to do?' she said quietly.

She was trembling.

'You're not going,' he whispered, panting. 'Sit

38

down. If you try to get out, or make any noise, I'll . . .'

'You'll what?'

'Sit down,' he whispered, hardly able to utter the words.

She moved backwards to her chair. She dropped her coat and cap once more on to the table. Then he left the door and approached her.

'Kitty,' he said, 'I'm sorry, but . . . Don't aggravate me. Do you hear? It's a matter of . . . I can't tell you, but you must do what I want you to do.'

'Madman.'

'Do you hear?'

She burst into a peal of hysterical laughter.

'What is it?' he said.

'God! You look so funny . . . like a walking corpse.'

They became silent, looking at one another.

'Supposing she has turned traitor,' thought McDara. 'Why did I send for her? Now she knows I'm here. What's to be done?'

His attitude suddenly changed. He assumed a pathetic expression, intending to play on her pity. At all costs he must get her to help him.

He went to the fire, drew up a chair and sat down. He put his head in his hands and drew in a deep breath. He remained like that, taut, shuddering, like a man struggling with a violent crisis.

She watched him for several moments, examining his sordid clothes, his emaciated frame, his quivering limbs. Then she shuddered. He produced the desired effect on her. A tear came into her right eye and trickled down her cheek. She wiped it away and approached him. She put her hands on his shoulders.

'What is it, Michael?' she said. 'Tell me. Forgive me for being cruel to you. Tell me. Is it true that you are a spy? Do tell me. Why do you treat me like this?'

She in turn broke down and went on her knees beside him in front of the fire. She began to sob.

'Oh! Why is everything so hopeless . . . everybody so cruel? . . . I wish I were dead.'

She buried her head in his lap and sobbed. Her fit of pity had been short-lived and her previous instinct of curiosity had again overcome her. She now wanted to get him to tell her what he intended to do.

McDara looked down at her with set teeth.

'Curse her,' he thought. 'I'll have to tell her. But is she to be trusted? Eh? But I must get her to help. This is awful.'

He put out his hand and touched her black hair that was now disordered. The silkiness of its touch stirred a faint desire in him. He raised his hand hurriedly as if he had touched a flame. The desire died immediately and he opened his lips in a strange grin.

She raised her head suddenly and looked at him. Now there were no tears in her eyes.

'Are you going to tell me?' she said.

Her long white neck, thrown back, was close to his face. He could see down her breasts, within her dress. That excited him again. He frowned and thrust her away from him. She refused to move and clung to his knees.

'What do you want me to tell you?' he said.

'What have you been doing for the past three years?'

He paused, contorted his face and then blurted out:

'All right, damn it. I'll tell you. Sit down. I can't talk to you like this. I don't want to start all over again.'

'Start what?' she said demurely.

He looked at her throat, down into her breasts. She got to her feet, putting her hand over her throat.

'I thought you said you were no longer interested in women,' she said.

She brought up another chair and sat down.

'Well?' she said.

'Well?' he answered in an angry voice. 'I put out those rumours myself. I cut adrift when I escaped from jail three years ago because . . . because I decided to do a certain thing.'

'What's that?'

'Eh? I cut adrift because I decided that all you people are no good. No damn good. A gang of humbugs, wasters, self-seekers. I decided to act on my own.'

'In what way?'

He looked at her again. Again, he had a horrible suspicion that she was a spy trying to drag his secret out of him. He looked at her so fiercely that she shuddered before his gaze.

'I don't trust you,' he said suddenly.

'I like that coming from you,' she said.

'Ach!' he said. 'What does that matter? When a man has in mind . . . Hell!'

He stopped again and clutched her by the arm.

'I must tell you,' he muttered, 'that what I am going to do is so important that I'd shoot you like a dog if I thought you'd ever utter one word.'

She nodded her head and said:

'I believe you now.'

'Will you help me?'

'Yes.'

'Are you still active?'

'As far as anybody can be said to be active.'

'How is that?'

'The country is rotten.'

'I know that. But are you in touch with people?'

'Yes.'

'Well. I want you to get a man for me and then . . . certain information.'

'What information?'

'I'll tell you that afterwards.'

'You'll have to tell me first what you're going to do. Otherwise I won't budge.'

42

'Eh?' he cried, starting violently. 'How do you mean?'

She was looking at him coldly, with a look of malice in her grey eyes.

'Curse it,' he thought, 'she'll insist on dragging it out of me. Must I tell her?'

Perspiration stood out on his forehead. He passed his hand over his skull, ruffling his scraggy fair hair and tearing at it.

'I know it,' she cried suddenly.

He looked at her in surprise. Her eyes were wide open, with the innocent look of a young girl. She was looking up at him with enthusiastic eagerness.

'I know it,' she repeated. 'You are going to kill . . .'

He opened his lips as if to finish the sentence for her. But he remained silent. They both looked at one another in silence, with their mouths open. Through a common instinct they both started and looked around the room. Then McDara closed his mouth and raised his shoulders. His eyes gleamed fiercely. She grew pale and began to tremble.

'Isn't that so?' she said in a whisper.

He made no movement. His eyes became fixed.

'Tell me, tell me,' she whispered excitedly.

Her nostrils were twitching. He raised his clenched fists to a level with his shoulders and swelled out his lungs. Then he closed his eyes and writhed as if in great pain.

Then he uttered an oath.

She threw her arms around his neck and whispered with her lips close to his:

'It will be a holy act.'

He began to mutter:

'One word and I'll shoot you like a dog.'

CHAPTER FOUR

AFTER she had gone, McDara began to experience the mental torture of the conspirator. Until now, the idea had lain hidden in his brain, perfectly secure, known only to Fetch. And Fetch was a man whom it was not necessary to fear, an automaton, upon whose senses he could play as on a flute. Now, however, the existence of his plan had been whispered by his lips into a woman's ear. It had grown from an idea, formless, without substance, into something heavy and irksome, like a child in a woman's womb. He suspected the very air that had carried the whispered words into her ear.

As he stood within the door of his room, listening to her departing steps going down the stairs, a sickly moisture rose up through his hair.

Eh? Had he been heard whispering to her by some slit-eyed spy stooping by the keyhole? Was she to be trusted? Did she dream at night? Would they suddenly arrest her and torture her?

He locked the door and put his fingers in his ears, to drive her altogether out of his consciousness. He didn't want to hear her bang the street door after her. But he immediately took out his fingers again and listened intently, waiting to hear her bang the door. Bang! He felt shut in, in prison, while she stole away to tell the police. He felt a desire to rush to the window and hurl himself down upon her. Then he raised his hands to his face, sighed heavily, went to the water-tap and put his mouth under it. He swallowed a deep draught of the running water. Then he stripped off his clothes and went to bed.

He got up again, lit the gas and examined the linen band about his waist. He felt, with his fingers, the little bundles of notes in the pockets. They were secure. Again he turned off the light and got into bed.

He closed his eyes and tried to sleep. That was impossible. When he began to doze he was startled by a strange, instinctive, imaginary movement of his hands. He felt his hands were reaching out to clutch Kitty Mellett by the throat and smother his secret in her before she could impart it.

This was beyond control of his reason. His reasoning mind remained calm. It summoned all its forces to combat these senseless fears, lest they might drive him into a panic and ruin everything. He swelled out his lungs and stooped forward as if to ram them with his head.

Still they came again and again. When he fell asleep, he kept pursuing her over the brink of a precipice. She had a document in her hand and she was waving it to some one down below.

Next morning, when he awoke, his body was bathed in perspiration. He sat up in bed and said aloud, in fright:

'Where is she?'

Then he struck his forehead and regained control of himself.

46

'At eight o'clock. At the corner of the lane. Yes. Eight o'clock.'

He felt at ease, after reminding himself that she said she would come at eight o'clock to the corner of the lane. He got up, cooked his breakfast and ate it. He put on his cap and raincoat to go out; but as he was going to the door another thought struck him.

'Had anyone been listening at the door while she was here?'

He took off his cap and coat, sat down at the table and decided to wait until the servant came into the room to make the bed. He would know by her manner if she had heard anything. He pretended to be writing letters.

She entered the room. She started when she saw him sitting at the table, looking at her with his terrible sunken eyes. 'Beg pardon, sir,' she said.

'That's all right,' he answered. 'Go ahead.'

He watched her as she fumbled clumsily about the room. Her loud asthmatic breathing mingled with some vague mutterings that came from her lips like an everlasting curse on life. Watching her, he felt an extraordinary hatred for her, just because she was a human being. Now all human beings were potential enemies. He felt glad that she was ugly and stupid and had asthma that sapped her energies. She would not ferret about. He had nothing to fear from her.

Again he put on his cap and raincoat and left the

room. But as he was going down the stairs he thought of his landlady. Had she been listening? Why not? A soldier's widow. 'One never knows what these women are connected with. This country is a network of spies. It always was.' His hands made the same imaginary, instinctive movements as they had made during the night. This time it was the landlady's throat they wanted to clutch. Then his cunning came to the rescue and he decided to visit the landlady about his laundry.

He went along the passage into the kitchen. He found her there, wrapped in an old dressing-gown, sitting by a table near the fire, reading the morning paper and drinking a cup of tea. Somehow, he was glad to see that she was sitting idly by the fire instead of being at her work. There was an air of sensuality about her that pleased him. She looked up when she saw him and he thought he saw a slight smile on her heavy lips.

'Sorry for disturbing you, Mrs. Buggy,' he said. 'I wanted to make some arrangements about my laundry. Is it called for here or do I have to take it out myself?'

'Just parcel it up,' she said, 'and leave it in the hall. Mondays.'

'Oh! Thanks very much,' he said.

He paused for a moment. She was looking at him. A subtle thought came into his head. As quick as lightning he shot a glance at her, with all his force, an amorous glance. He held her dark eyes and

looked at her with the shameless, lewd ferocity of
passion. She started slightly and then, after a little
pause, returned his glance. He smiled faintly and
turned on his heel, guided by the same subtle
instinct not to press his attentions any further just
then. He rubbed his hands gleefully going out the
hall.

'That'll work,' he thought.

He pulled his cap aslant over his forehead, buttoned up his raincoat and set off down the street.
He now felt in a state of intense happiness. He
reached the corner of Parnell Square and turned
southwards. Just there he collided with a policeman
who was going northwards with a cape over his
shoulder. McDara almost jumped clean off the
street and then stood still, paralysed with fright.
Had the policeman been waiting for him, waiting to
grab him?

The tall policeman muttered a gruff oath and
looked at the fellow who had bumped against him.
He saw a lean, skimpy man, with sunken eyes and
a deadly pale forehead, hollow pale cheeks with
vertical lines in them, stooping shoulders, dressed
in a shabby raincoat. He growled contemptuously
at this shabby outcast and said:

'Why the hell don't ye mind where yer goin'?'

Then he walked on growling.

McDara also moved on, trembling at the knees.
But his mind was laughing with a sudden access of
extraordinary glee. As if by magic, this physical

encounter with the policeman had brought into being a force in his mind that had until then remained dormant. Or was it the IDEA come to life?

He walked on, looking in upon himself, wondering. He was aware of being two people.

One was terror-stricken, eagerly watching for enemies, acutely conscious of the most minute details of life, smelling, looking, listening, reacting to every touch in an abandoned manner. The consciousness of this personality had become sharpened to an exasperating degree. It had established itself in separate quarters in his brain and was feverishly busy marshalling thoughts and impressions covering the whole expanse of existence. It was a genius, capable of conjuring up, with exciting vividness, emotions, passions and brilliant inspirations, all of them awe-inspiring. It had a feminine attribute, because it was negative, hysterical and cunning, preying on his other personality, just as a woman preys on her mate.

The other, new-born personality was masculine, a scoffing, arrogant, contemptuous one. With a bold, callous will, it caught and crushed every idea and suggestion that was offered to it, rummaged through it, plundered what was useful and cast out the remainder. This personality existed in his body like a foreigner. It despised his body.

He walked across the city brooding. He passed into a state of ecstasy. The city became transformed in his mind. Although he walked along the sordid,

commonplace thoroughfare of O'Connell Street, surrounded by noise, mud, ragged people and ugly
buildings, his inward-gazing thoughts fashioned a
thrilling and romantic panorama.

First came a fantasy that had inspired him in childhood. On the banks of the Po, when the dawn mists
were rising, Hasdrubal's Nubian cavalry, caparisoned, glittering with embroidered cloths, with
columns of smoke from their red, wide-opened
nostrils, came galloping, each carrying a dark, slim-
legged giant. The thunder of their hoofs resounded
on the river-banks. And louder than the thunder of
their galloping hoofs came the blare of long trumpets
sounding the battle charge.

He passed by the ruined buildings, relics of the
recent wars. A warm feeling rose up in his chest,
as when a man conceives a passionate desire for
a beloved, whom he soon hopes to ravish in his
arms.

He passed by the Nelson monument, unseeing,
walking gloomily with his eyes on the ground.

Now the houses of the city, the dark waters of
the foul, sewage-bearing river and the people who
passed, loomed large in his vision and became transformed, signalling to his imagination a myriad
speechless signs. From all corners of the land came
peasants marching, with blood on their waving
banners, into the capital, into the fortress of the
tyrant, who had been struck down in death, by the
hand and brain of Michael McDara. A head! THE

51

HEAD! With blood-stained, yellow lips and a scattered brain.

As he walked, gazing at the ground, thinking thus exultantly, his terrified humanity babbled a ceaseless stream of weird suggestions, overwhelmed by the size of the load it carried. But his mind scoffed at these fears.

All morning, he walked round and round, in and out, through the streets bordering on the river. At half-past twelve, he suddenly felt exhausted and very hungry. He turned northwards towards the spot where he was to meet Fetch at two o'clock. He passed the betting shop where he had an appointment with Fetch and entered a cheap eating-house.

When he entered the place it was crowded and he had to stand by the fire waiting for a seat. The majority of the people who were eating there were workmen of a poor class. He noticed one man sitting on the edge of a deal form near the fire. This man was obviously not a workman and McDara conceived a strange suspicion of him. He began to watch the man. Then he thought the man was watching him.

The fellow was a stocky man, with an ape-like face, full of wrinkles and as yellow as parchment. His ears protruded from the sides of his skull. He wore his hat while he ate and also his overcoat. His overcoat was the most curious thing about him. It bunched out behind the back of his neck, like a hump. It was of a light brown colour, spotted with little blobs of grey wool, like an animal's hide. The man ate ravenously, wrinkling his forehead and moving his jaws and throat violently, as if he expected to choke with each gobble. He looked at McDara several times and also at the proprietor of the place, who was standing beside McDara.

McDara began to perspire with nervousness. Gradually the eaters paid their score and left the room. McDara sat down at the same table as the man with the ape-like face. He ordered a meal of beef and potatoes. He began to eat very slowly. He wanted the other fellow to clear out before he left himself.

The ape-like man, with the hump on his overcoat, finished his meal and lit a cigarette. He became still more suspicious in McDara's eyes. He made furtive movements with his hands about his person, feeling the pockets of his overcoat and also those of his trousers under the table. The proprietor was now watching him.

McDara fumbled with his food, unable to swallow anything, because he now felt sure that both the proprietor and the man with the hump on his overcoat were watching him, waiting to arrest him.

'She has given the game away,' he thought. 'That fellow came in here to trap me.'

Then he felt relieved, thinking that nobody knew he was coming in here. He was on the point of shouting out to the ape-like man to ask him what did he mean by staring that way, when the latter

53

individual suddenly got to his feet. The proprietor advanced at the same moment and stood behind McDara. McDara caught his fork in a tight grip and was on the point of jumping up to defend himself, when the ape-like man bounded across the table, making for the door.

'Catch the devil,' yelled the proprietor to McDara.

McDara stooped instead of catching the man as he crossed the table. In a moment the ape-like man had darted out the door, pursued by the proprietor.

'Catch him,' yelled the proprietor. 'He's gone without paying. Steak an' onions an' rice pudding.'

McDara put his elbows on the table and burst into a peal of hysterical laughter. His face was wet with perspiration.

After a few minutes the proprietor came back, panting and still swearing wildly. He stood within the door, rubbing his fat stomach.

'He got away on me,' he cried. 'He got away.'

Then he burst forth into a torrent of oaths. McDara got up, paid his score and left the place. He walked hurriedly down the street until he came to the betting shop.

He stood on the opposite side of the narrow street watching it, afraid to enter, because it was yet only half-past one and he thought it might arouse suspicions if he were seen hanging around there for half an hour.

The shop had a more luxurious front than any

other shop in the mean street. The name over the door, TUTTY, TURF ACCOUNTANT, was done in ornate yellow lettering. It had a glass window covering the whole front. In the window there were several tablets, giving the prospective runners for important races and the prices at which the horses were on that day quoted in London. In the upper part of the window there was a huge cheque, like an illuminated address, with the motto, PAY BEARER ONE THOUSAND POUNDS, M. TUTTY. A group of people were leaning against the window of the shop, arguing and consulting racing papers. A thin man, with his overcoat unbuttoned, stood in front of this group on the pavement and made movements with his hands and legs as if he were riding a horse in a race. Then he finished riding the imaginary horse, threw his cap in the air and cried out loud enough for McDara to hear: 'Ten to one. Won by a street. Only himself in it an' the jockey lookin' back.' The group of men paid no heed to the thin man's story, but he went eagerly from one to the other of them, pointing his finger and gesticulating like a crazy person.

Suddenly, something important happened within the shop. The group of men standing against the window rushed in the door, pushing one another. Several other men, whom McDara had not noticed standing about, came across the street at a run and disappeared into the shop. Two old women came out of a lane to the right, wiping their hands in their aprons. McDara looked up the lane and saw a piece

THE ASSASSIN

of red cloth, a blanket, hanging on a line, drawn
across the end of the lane in a courtyard. The old
women had been washing there.

His curiosity was aroused and he also went across
the street. He entered the shop but he could get no
farther than the door. It was closely packed with
people. They were all babbling. The result of a race
had just been announced when he reached the door.
The people were pushing their way out again, some
cursing, others laughing and acting similarly to the
thin man who had been gesticulating outside. All
sorts of people went past him, women and men, but
on all their faces there was the same look of feverish
exaltation, whether of joy or of despair.

Crouching against the wall, in order to let the
crowd pass out, he also became exalted. He felt a
kinship with these mad gamblers. The terrors of the
morning had awakened a sentimental desire for sym-
pathy in him. And when man feels weak and timid,
it is then that he broods lovingly over misery, sin,
death and the violent salvation of upheaval.

So now, leaning against the wall, he contemplated
with dark joy the madness and debauchery of man,
gambling, leching and carousing, while the civiliza-
tion wrought by centuries of his labour crumbled
about his ears. As if sin were necessary to the birth
of Christ. He rejoiced darkly, seeing the tumult of
passion about him, the degraded souls gambling,
while the country was being laid waste by the
tyrant. So . . . the blow would come like a thunder-

56

bolt among them. It would come striding out of the heavens in a flash, sudden, awe-inspiring.

Fumes of passion rose up through his body to his head. He became dizzy. Tears came into his eyes and he suddenly longed to lie down and cry aloud for pity. He saw his mother's face, standing afar off, holding out her thin hands to him, beseeching him to come to her bosom. And he remembered she was dead. Then he saw his home on a mountain slope with the sea beyond. The smells and sounds of his childhood became so sweet that his bowels suffered an agony of longing. Then he saw death, on all sides, engulfing man and a horrible void beyond, terrible with fierce cries of anguish, with hands clawing the emptiness and fleshless lips constantly murmuring: 'Where? Where? There is nothing.'

His mouth had opened. His lips had drawn back from his teeth. He had begun to faint. A man carrying an attaché-case was approaching from the counter to the ledge against the wall, where bets were written on slips of paper. This man, a stout, well-dressed man, with glasses, saw McDara. He halted and looked at McDara with interest. Immediately, McDara recovered and looked at the man fiercely. The man turned away and went to the ledge. McDara's mind became calm. He stood erect against the wall and looked about the shop. His mind had suddenly become empty and cold.

Now there were only a few people in the shop.

Behind the counter, two clerks were standing, working at papers. One was a little fellow, with a smiling face. His fair hair was glossy with oil. The other man was tall, with a strong face and a large nose. He had a newly lit cigar in his mouth. A ragged, dirty man was going about the floor, picking up slips of paper and examining them. In the corner there was a telephone with a curtain about it. At the far end of the room there was a board, with the name of an English race-course written on the top, and, underneath, the names and prices of the horses that had won the first two races of the day. There was a rank odour of tobacco in the room. There was also a heavy smell of humanity, a sickening smell.

McDara became aware that it was this smell that had made him feel weak. And he thought: 'I must be careful. I don't want to break down until the job is done.'

The shop began to fill again with people. It was nearing two o'clock. A loud babbling of voices reached his ears. Again people pushed against him, going to the ledge where bets were written out. He was crushed against the wall and a feeling of terrible despair overcame him. 'What can be done? There is nothing. What do they seek? What do I seek? There is only death?'

'Runners,' cried the ragged man, pushing his way down the room from the telephone booth, with a tablet in his hand. 'One, three, four down to ten, fifteen, twenty-two, twenty-five.'

'Is eleven not runnin'?' cried a voice. 'Blast an' curse it, anyway.'

'Runners,' cried the ragged man again. 'One, three, four down to ten, fifteen . . .'

The mob rushed to the counter with their slips. A fury seized them. The hands, holding aloft the slips to the man who smoked the long cigar, were trembling with excitement. Lips babbled silent words. A woman, with a baby in her arms, pushed her way in, holding a slip of dirty paper in which money was rolled. She was followed by a bearded tramp, who was wearing two overcoats. There was a smell from the tramp and people moved away from him, as he pushed his way up to the counter. A carter, with a whip in his belt, was pushed back near to McDara. Breathing heavily, he whispered to McDara that he got Sprig for the Grand National and that if Orbindos did the trick he could be drunk until the sun went down in Maryland. A man with a tattered hat put a cigarette into his mouth, struck a match and then let the match go out. The cigarette hung from his lower lip. The tramp came back from the counter, rubbing his black hands, shaking his beard and smiling all round him. Suddenly, the oily-haired clerk ran over to the tinkling telephone in the corner. He shouted out:

'All gone.'

'They're off,' croaked the tramp. 'Now for the man with hair on his chest. Tare an' ouns.'

The betting shop became as silent as a tomb. All

59

stood still, like wax figures, as if struck dead in in-congruous attitudes by the sudden rush of horses from a white tape, three hundred miles away in England. Walled in, within that stinking room, their minds envisaged the green turf and the glossy forms of the horses, ridden by gaudy jockeys, flash-ing past like swallows on the wing, with their bellies to earth. Their faces were like screens on which demons were drawing images of all the human passions.

The big man, standing behind the counter, con-tinued to smoke his long cigar. He had his elbow on the counter. His closed fist was against his jaw, pushing against the cigar. Columns of smoke rose from his mouth. His bored eyes glanced around the room contemptuously.

Another man, with a glossy face and a body like a barrel, stood at the door, tapping his teeth with a pencil. He had a slip of paper in his hand. Spas-modically, the hand holding the paper jerked up-wards and he whispered: 'Tillyvally. Tillyvally.'

The telephone tinkled. In a low voice the oily-haired clerk called out the winner.

'What? What won? What?'

'Be the jumpin' God!' exclaimed the tramp.

He leaped clean off the floor and dug his elbows into the sides of those near him.

'One hundred to eight,' said the oily-haired clerk.

'One hundred to eight,' yelled the tramp. 'It's money for jam.'

McDara heard Fetch whispering into his ear. He started. Fetch had suddenly appeared beside him. Fetch's nostrils were twitching. He looked wild. He jerked his head and walked out. McDara followed him. Outside in the street, Fetch caught McDara's arm and said excitedly:

'Come on away. I want to talk to you.'

They went down the street, crossed over to O'Connell Bridge and boarded a Phœnix Park tram. They climbed to the top. They sat at the front of the tram. They were alone there.

'Listen,' said Fetch hurriedly. 'Unless you hustle with this job I'm goin' out on my own.'

CHAPTER FIVE

KITTY MELLETT left McDara's lodgings in a state of
ecstasy. Her mind was void of thought. She was
contemplating the vision of a female spirit in flowing
robes, Ireland, whom she was about to free from
bondage.

It was not yet ten o'clock. This was the best time
to go to look for the man whom McDara wanted.
McDara had begged her to hurry. But she set off
homewards. She wanted one night alone with her
great secret.

Smiling dreamily, with her eyes on the ground,
lifting her feet up high like a person in a trance, she
went by back streets, across the river at Butt Bridge
and then through dark lanes until she reached her
mother's house in a quiet square near Ballsbridge.
She entered by the wicket gate in a lane at the rear of
the house. She went on tiptoe through the garden
plot. She unlatched the kitchen door and stole up
the back stairs to her room without being seen
by anybody. Goodness only knows why she went
through all this hide-and-seek business, as there was
positively no necessity for it; but it gave her great
pleasure. When she got into her room, she locked
the door, took off her cap and raincoat and then sat
on her bed, with a weary gesture. Folding her arms
on her breast, she stared at the floor, still smiling
dreamily.

It was a bare, dreary room. There was no carpet

on the floor, no fire in the grate, no furniture except a wardrobe, one chair and the bed. It was bitterly cold. She had eaten nothing since midday. Yet, she was neither cold nor hungry. She remained in a state of exalted ecstasy, void of thought.

Now she did not look beautiful. Her face was hard. Her eyes were brilliant, fixed and cruel. They had the vicious, cold look that is seen in the eyes of a child tearing a doll. After a while, her mind began to create thoughts. Then she became aware of the cold. She got up and paced the room. Thinking, she was also happy. What was about to be done arose in her mind in relation to herself alone. It would be her gesture of revenge. By that act she would have revenge for all the contumelies ever suffered by her. According to her mind, she had a long score against life. Indeed, it appeared to her mind that this act had come straight from the hand of Providence, at the very moment when she was about to give up hope of ever being able to revenge herself.

She had now been nine years in the revolutionary movement. She joined at the age of nineteen. She had been carried away by the general enthusiasm, which at that time had mysteriously gripped the people. She became enamoured of the 'white-robed prisoner' just at the age when she was waking to the attractions of the other sex. By that act she had cut herself adrift from her family. Her father was a solicitor, holding an important position under the

Imperial Government. He was a Conservative Unionist, bitterly hostile to the Republican cause. He died shortly after Kitty became a rebel, saying that the disgrace had killed him. As a matter of truth, he died of kidney trouble. The other six members of his family obeyed his wise counsel and did well for themselves. The boys entered the Imperial Civil Service. The two girls married Imperial army officers. They were all living out of Ireland, most of them in the Imperial possessions east of Suez. They had no interest in Ireland and held no communication with Kitty. They even cut off communication with their mother, because she allowed Kitty to go on living in the house.

Mrs. Mellett hated Kitty and would long since have got rid of her, were it not for a provision in her husband's will. He had left Mrs. Mellett an annuity of four hundred and fifty pounds and out of this sum she was to take care of his 'erring daughter.' The old woman, unable to persuade her daughter to leave the revolutionary movement, persecuted her, starved her, never gave her any money, took the carpet off her bedroom floor and stored away her bedroom furniture in the garret.

While the revolutionary movement was in triumph, Kitty had been indifferent to these 'contumelies,' as she called them. She was an officer in a large women's army. She wore a green uniform. She carried arms. She marched and drilled. She went to jail. She was acclaimed in the streets by mobs as a popular hero. She travelled secretly over the country carrying arms and dispatches. She reviewed battalions of women fighters. She took part in plots and even raided shops and held up enemies at the point of the revolver.

But suddenly all that vanished. The women's army vanished. The country fell into a state of apathy, after the treaty with England, the Civil War and the rout of the Republicans. Now, instead of a great army of women, with uniforms and guns, there was merely a tiny organization of one hundred disgruntled old maids, seeking revenge for the strange trick played on them by fate. All the young and pretty ones had left. There remained only those who were unwanted virgins and a few like Kitty, who was the unfortunate possessor of a temperament that could not attune itself to reality. Even in this tiny organization she was regarded with suspicion and would undoubtedly have been expelled for heretical views, were it not for the fact that the executive never met.

As she wandered around the room, Kitty desired revenge on these old maids more than on anybody else. And curiously enough, the thought of revenge on HIM, who was doomed to die, never once entered her mind.

Then she undressed and crept into her cold bed. In bed, her feverish enthusiasm vanished. She felt weak and timid and lonely. She began to weep. Then she fell asleep.

Next morning she awoke in a mood of depression, as she had been in the habit of doing of late. But almost immediately she remembered that she must find Tumulty. That cheered her. At last there was something definite to do. She arose at once and dressed carefully. She put on her best clothes. Her wardrobe was well stocked in spite of her poverty. Rich women connected with the movement supplied her with clothes. As she was the only attractive woman left, she was always given the job of getting information. For this purpose good clothes were necessary. She put on an expensive fur coat over her dress.

Feeling good clothes on her body, with a set purpose in her mind, she felt strong and happy. She decided, before going out, to begin her revenge on her mother. So she went down into the kitchen. The old woman was sitting there, nagging at her servant. Kitty stood within the door, with her legs widespread, in a masculine attitude. She said in an arrogant voice that she did not want any breakfast that morning.

The old woman turned around. She was small and withered, with white hair, little narrow eyes that had no colour in them and hands like claws.

'I don't care,' she mumbled, speaking very slowly, 'if I never set eyes on you again. Now then, Biddy, get on with your work. You have no time to gawk. Your absence, Kitty, is always better than your presence. Now then.'

66

Kitty lingered by the door, full of rage and chagrin. Whenever she came into her mother's presence, a feeling of having injured her mother irritated her and made her feel unhappy and mean. However, just because of that feeling, she determined to stay badgering her mother, in order to 'vindicate' herself.

'If anybody calls,' she said, 'say I won't be back until very late.'

'I never speak to your friends,' snapped the old woman. 'You and your friends have soured my old age. I spent my youth struggling with poverty. You sent your poor father to his grave. This is my reward for skimping and saving. When the hive was full you scattered the honey. Biddy, you slut, that toast is burning.'

'If I'm not back to-night you needn't be anxious about me,' said Kitty.

The old woman got furious.

'Clear out,' she screamed. 'You rip. You disgraceful girl.'

Kitty laughed and walked away. There were tears of self-pity in her eyes, when she got into the street.

'Why must I go on like this?' she thought. 'It's all wrong. I'm a fool. A fool.'

She went towards Kathleen O'Mara's house, a few streets away. It was a tall, red-brick house, divided into flats. The top flat was occupied by Miss O'Mara herself. The remainder of the house was occupied by her friends, generally cranks who were associated at one time or another with the nationalist revolutionary movement. They hardly ever paid her any rent. They came and went, without contract or licence, just as they pleased. The place was continually being raided and Miss O'Mara enjoyed that very much. She had money of her own and chose this sort of Bohemian, conspiratorial life, as the best means of amusing herself. She was a thin, anæmic woman, but she had a great reputation in the movement. She had been on hunger strike three times. She had taken part in very daring adventures, of a spectacular and public nature. She was reputed to have prophetic powers and claimed to have been in spiritual communication with long-deceased Irish patriots. Thus, although she had neither brains nor ability of a practical sort, she was considered to be an important national leader, by her own followers. The fact that she had money and was generous with it was perhaps largely responsible for her reputation. And it is also very curious, that although she hated England violently, her income came from investments in Ceylon, where English capitalists were exploiting native labour to supply Kathleen O'Mara with money for helping to free Ireland from English Imperialism. Such are the contradictions of life.

Kitty knocked at the door and was admitted by the caretaker, a stout woman of forty, with a florid face and big, dark eyes. This woman's husband had been shot during the Civil War. Her business as a huckster had broken up as a result of his death. She was employed by Kathleen O'Mara purely from sentimental reasons, as she was useless as a worker, owing to her liking for drink. But . . . What a human being! She was worth ten women. Big in heart and body, she had a voice like a grumbling sea and a laugh that could shake a door off its hinges. She swore with every sentence. She treated everybody with arrogant familiarity. When she had a couple of drinks, she went into the streets and told the public that the Government was composed of 'murderers,' 'drunken wasters' and 'lead-roof robbers.' She was typical of the REAL fighting Irishwoman of the common people, of the same breed that had defended Limerick; the nameless ones.

'Where's yer hurry?' she bawled out when she saw Kitty.

'Is Miss O'Mara up yet?' said Kitty.

'Indeed she's not,' said the caretaker. 'What'd she be doin' up at this hour? Go on up, though. You'll find her. Is it cold out?'

Kitty went up to the top floor and knocked at the door of Miss O'Mara's flat. After some time, a tall, thin woman, with prominent teeth, came out, wearing a dressing-gown over a long white nightdress. It was Kathleen O'Mara.

'May I come in and have breakfast with you?' said Kitty.

'Yes, do come in,' said Miss O'Mara, in a sleepy voice.' I'm just awake. You're out early.'

'Yes. I'm busy. I want breakfast and information, if you can give it to me.'

Kathleen O'Mara's eyes opened wide with excitement. She took Kitty by the arm and drew her into the sitting-room. She closed the door and turned on the electric fire. Then she crouched over the fire on a low stool.

'Has anything happened?' she said excitedly.

'Nothing particular,' said Kitty with a yawn, as she took off her coat.

'I'm sure something has happened,' said Kathleen. 'Now, be a sport, Kitty. What is it?'

'Well,' said Kitty, 'I'm looking for somebody. First, I want breakfast, though. I'm very hungry. Shall I cook it?'

'Yes, do,' said Kathleen. 'But tell me first.'

Kitty paused and then said mysteriously:

'Well, it's nothing important really. I have a message for a man called Tumulty. He was in the volunteers, but I think he has dropped out. Do you know him?'

'Let me see,' said Kathleen. 'I can't place him. I seem to have heard the name somewhere, though. I can't remember. I say, though, Kitty, you have something on hand. Tell me.'

'You don't know the man?'

'No. I'm sorry. But tell me, though. I'm positive you're on some job.'

'Wait till we have breakfast.'

Kitty went to the kitchenette and began to cook

breakfast. Kathleen, shivering in her dressing-gown, followed her about, asking questions. Kitty kept putting her off. They had breakfast. Kitty ate with a good appetite. Kathleen just drank tea and nibbled at a piece of toast.

When she had finished eating, Kitty got to her feet.

'I must go now,' she said mysteriously. 'I'm in a hurry.'

'Where are you going?' said Kathleen.

'Oh! I have a lot of things to do.'

'Oh! Do tell me,' said Kathleen, beginning to become hysterical with curiosity.

Kitty pursed up her lips and smiled faintly.

'You're a mean cat,' snapped Kathleen.

'Sorry, dear,' said Kitty with a sigh.

Suddenly Kathleen threw her arms around Kitty's neck and whispered:

'Do let me help, Kitty. I'm so bored.'

'Later perhaps,' said Kitty.

'Yes, yes,' said Kathleen excitedly. 'Do. Do. I'll wait. Try Fred Corbett. He'll probably know something about the fellow. You're a lucky devil, Kitty. Oh! I'm dying to know what it is.'

Kitty put on her coat in silence. Then Kathleen lost her temper completely, because her curiosity could not be satisfied. She sat down on her stool and said contemptuously:

'How can I be such a fool? I too often try to deceive myself with the idea that I'm carrying the fate of the nation in my hands. But it wears off. I hope you find your Tulty or whoever he is . . . if he really exists. How boring!'

'That's so,' said Kitty, with a subtle smile.

Kathleen was too vexed to say good-bye. Kitty went out, feeling the delicious feminine pleasure of having excited another woman's jealousy and curiosity. She hurried down the stairs.

There was a loud noise of conversation in the flat on the second floor. The door stood ajar. She looked in, paused and then advanced to the sitting-room door. She knocked at the half-open door and entered. She was saluted by a loud shout of welcome. A crowd of men and women was sitting around the table having breakfast. There was a large dish full of sausages in the centre of the table. They invited her, with loud shouts, to sit down and have some sausages.

Kitty knew these people but she despised them. They were the dilettanti of the movement, freaks whom Kathleen O'Mara gathered about her, in order to persuade herself that she had a mass following. These people wandered around Dublin, living from hand to mouth, laughing, singing and roystering, incapable of doing anything useful, either for themselves or for the country. They had all done something years ago and they were living on their reputations, which were largely concocted by their own imaginations. However, they were very gay, unscrupulous and charming people.

One man jumped up when he saw Kitty. He came

towards her, waving his arms. His name was Fred Dignum. He had been tortured in jail six years previously and had since been a nervous wreck. Almost a genius, he could talk fluently about every conceivable subject, but he was incapable of making any use of his talents. He always insulted everybody, owing to a nervous instinct to overcome the contempt in which he believed he was held by everybody. His wild, blue eyes, his trembling hands, his pale, twitching face aroused a strange feeling of pity and repulsion in all that saw him. He had an uncanny faculty for reading people's minds; not directly, but at an oblique angle, as it were; just like a madman, who sees a portion of the most intricate idea much sooner than a sane person but is incapable of seeing the simplest thing in its full proportions.

'Hello! Hello!' he cried. 'You're Kitty Mellett. I know you hate me. But still . . . Now, don't interrupt. You think you are saving Ireland. Don't you? Now, I don't believe it. I think you are quite wrong and that you should be locked up or forcibly married.'

'Sit down, Fred, for God's sake!' somebody shouted.

'Don't interrupt me,' he cried. 'Look at her blush. She knows it's the truth. I say. All you people are merely the backwash of revolution. We all are. Anybody that had any intelligence joined the Government. Ha! ha! You can't bring a dead horse back to life by whipping the carcass. The peasants

73

have got all they want. The peasants won't fight.
They don't want a republic. The priests . . . yes,
the priests. . . . What are you going to do with the
priests? We are a hopeless lot. You know that. You
are all priest-ridden. A lot of sex complexes . . . I
mean . . . did you ever read Freud? Why don't
you read Freud or even Havelock Ellis?'

'Sit down or I'll throw a chair at you. Don't
mind him, Kitty. He's mad. Have a sausage.'

'No, thanks. I'm in a hurry. Good-bye.'

She went out. Dignum rushed after her, shouting
out her name. The others yelled at him to come
back. He called down the stairs after Kitty:

'There's not one of you has the courage to do it,
although you'd all love to have somebody do it.
There's one man standing in the way and you're
afraid to knock him out. He has the only brain in
the Government. But you're afraid because you
haven't the moral courage. You won't do it unless
somebody comes and does it for you and then you'll
let him down.'

Kitty halted at the angle of the stairs and whispered angrily:

'You'll get a bullet yet, even though you are mad.'

Dignum ran down a few paces and then began to
call out hysterically:

'It's not you, Kitty. I'm speaking symbolically of
the nationalist idea. It's full of complexes and ridden
by priests. It should be ridden by something else. I
say . . . I don't mean that, but . . .'

As she went out of sight, he leaned over the banisters, made a trumpet with his hands, laughed and yelled:

'The movement wants a strong man . . . in every sense of the word. . . . Ha! ha! In every sense, I say. . . . He! he!'

Somebody caught him by the throat and pulled him back.

Kitty almost cried with rage when she got out into the street. The crazy fellow's remarks had reminded her of her own doubts during the past months. Was it all hopeless after all?

For a long time she wandered about the streets, dazed and miserable, walking aimlessly. Then her depression wore off and she passed into an equally acute state of happiness. She continued to wander about, but now she was conscious of wandering with a purpose. She began to indulge in a favourite amusement of hers. She pretended to believe that she was followed by detectives. That was very pleasant.

At one o'clock she entered a restaurant frequented by revolutionaries. This was a rather secluded place, on the second floor of a bake-shop. There were two rooms and each was crowded. She passed through the front room, nodding to various people she knew. In the back room, she saw the man she wanted, sitting alone at a small table in the corner, eating some rice pudding and reading a book while he ate.

This man was Fred Corbett, a general in the secret volunteer army. He was hardly more than a youth,

75

perhaps twenty-three years of age. He had an extremely intelligent face, a strong jaw and a broad, straight back. He appeared to be a young man full of promise and yet there was something repellent in his expression and demeanour. It was that arrogant contemptuousness which seems to be characteristic of all revolutionaries; and is indeed characteristic of all young people who get a new idea into their heads. This young fellow was still a student at the university, but he had been a member of the volunteers since he was fifteen and had been in several serious engagements during the guerrilla wars. He had lately reached his present exalted rank owing to the rapid disintegration of the volunteer army. Indeed, the army, as a military force, existed more or less in his imagination and in the imaginations of his brother generals, who were as romantic as himself. But the smaller the army became and the less capable it became of taking part in any sort of campaign, the more arrogant became his opinion of its power and its future.

When Kitty saluted him, he looked up with a bored air, smiled faintly and prepared a chair for her beside him. She sat down and smiled at him in her most fascinating manner. He blushed slightly. His red cheeks, his boyish eyes with their serious, intellectual expression and his broad forehead made him look very handsome; but very like an innocent youth; not to be taken seriously.

'Well?' said Kitty. 'Any news?'

He shook his head and began to light a cigarette. The waitress came up. Kitty ordered her usual lunch, tea and bread and butter. They talked casually until the waitress had served the meal. Then Kitty leaned towards him and whispered in an indifferent tone:

'Tell me, do you know a man called Tumulty? Is he a volunteer? A friend of mine is looking for him and asked me to try and dig him up.'

Corbett's eyes narrowed and he said slowly:

'Yes. I know him. He's not a volunteer though. He's been expelled.'

'Is that so?' said Kitty, sipping her tea. 'Then I suppose . . .'

'Who wants to see him?' said Corbett quickly.

'Oh! A girl down the country,' said Kitty carelessly.

Then she looked up at Corbett suddenly in order to give a certain meaning to her words.

Corbett frowned and said contemptuously:

'H'm! I should think there would be . . . a girl looking for him. It's just the sort of thing I'd expect of him.'

The young general blew out a column of smoke and assumed an air of stern reproof. Obviously, he had nothing but contempt for Tumulty's moral character.

Kitty smiled. She was delighted at the cleverness with which she was 'winding this young pup around her fingers.' She would now be able to get her information without allowing him to suspect her purpose.

'You're very severe, Fred,' she said in a coy tone.

Corbett raised his eyebrows, shrugged his shoulders and sighed. Then he began to play with a little moustache he had begun to cultivate.

'What was he expelled for?' said Kitty carelessly.

'He's a disruptionist,' said Corbett. 'A rank disruptionist.'

'How?'

'How? Every way. One of those crazy fellows who are always looking for action, action, action. What we need is not action but organization, ideas, propaganda.'

'I see,' said Kitty, with a smile. 'You're too nice to get hurt, Fred.'

'How do you mean?' he said aggressively.

'Oh! Nothing,' said Kitty sweetly. 'Tell me, though. Where can I get hold of this bird? I don't want to let Lily . . . I mean could you give me his address?'

'Oh! Yes. I think so. Just a moment.'

He wrote it out on a slip of paper. She thanked him and put the slip of paper in her glove. Then her manner suddenly changed.

'Do you know,' she said in a nagging voice, 'I think you are an awful young humbug, Fred.'

'Eh?' he said, starting violently, as if somebody had struck him on the back.

She sipped her tea imperturbably.

78

'Really,' she said. 'It's not right at all.'

'What's not right?' he growled.

'Oh! Nothing at all,' she said coyly. 'But, you know, whenever I meet one of you fellows, I always think of the chocolate soldier. I don't mean the real chocolate soldier, but a soldier made of chocolate. Too soft to be touched, for fear he'd disrupt.'

Corbett said something under his breath and got to his feet.

'It's much better, you know,' she said in a low voice, 'to fight your battles around a table among your own generals than to . . .'

But he had fled before she could finish.

CHAPTER SIX

McDara looked in amazement at Fetch. Rocking from side to side, hurtling against one another with the movement of the tram-car, their faces were at one moment close together and at the next wide apart. This movement heightened the feeling of terror that was aroused in McDara by the strange, distraught appearance of Fetch. He could hardly believe his eyes. Fetch was panic-stricken.

The tram-car rumbled along the river-bank. The two men, sitting alone on the top of the vehicle, stood out against the horizon boldly, like marionettes in a puppet show, playing the part of madmen possessed by the Furies.

Having uttered his statement, Fetch remained silent, as if waiting for McDara to liberate him from his panic. McDara also remained silent, disconcerted, not so much by Fetch's words as by the look in his eyes. The scar on the man's face seemed to have become quite new and white.

'What the hell is biting you?' said McDara at last.

'Eh?' snapped Fetch.

Then he let loose a torrent of words.

'Listen,' he whispered tensely, his lips trembling as he spoke. 'I don't like the look of this proposition. I got a hunch that this is going to end in . . .' He made a circular movement with his forefinger around his throat. 'And yours truly has no hankering for a rope. Savvy? You got me in on this, Mac. Get busy an' let's get out of here. I'll do the job. You just say the word. That Judy put the wind up me. I don't like the look of her. And Tumulty no more. I played my own game. Savvy? I don't want any truck with these little craw-thumpers. I plugged some o' these Republicans. Savvy? I got a queer feeling around here. I don't like the smell o' this town. I see things around here. Come on. Let's get busy an' get out. I'm goin' to get that fellow first, though. He's goin' to pay [for me. By God! I'm goin' to send that fellow to hell before me an' I'll burn his hide for all eternity. He got me to crease a few fellahs. But nobody's goin' to call me a murderer. No, sir.'

'Eh?' said McDara.

The tram-conductor came upstairs to collect the fares. McDara produced three pence and handed them to the tram-conductor. The conductor handed him two tickets and went away. McDara looked at Fetch, clenched his teeth, grinned and said:

'This is great.'

Fetch's little eyes gleamed.

'I thought you said you didn't believe in God,' said McDara.

'Quit that,' said Fetch in a hoarse voice.

He seemed exhausted by his outburst. His lips hung open. His eyebrows were contracted. The scar on his cheek twitched. His queer, triangular face was in agony.

McDara continued to grin, looking straight into

81

Fetch's eyes. A strange feeling of power possessed him. An equally strange joy made him grin at the realization that he held this brute in his power, playing on his superstitious fears of the bloody deeds he had committed. And it seemed most fitting that Fetch, who had been the hired murderer of the tyrant, should be one of the tyrant's assassins.

He took Fetch by the arm and whispered to him quietly:

'Listen, Gutty. You remember when I was in camp, you used to come into my cell the first few days I was there in your charge and stick a gun into my mouth. You told me all you'd do to me. Well? What did I do? I just laughed at you. I knew what was biting you. I got your measure, old son. We were old comrades. I picked you up in a whore-house one night I was on the run. I took you away from your job. What was it? Pimping, wasn't it?'

'Let up on that,' growled Fetch.

'I put a gun in your hand,' continued McDara, 'and made you a hero, didn't I? Then you turned your coat and became a hired thug of the Government.'

'By God,' muttered Fetch, 'I'll turn again if you don't . . .'

'Chuck it,' sneered McDara. 'You've seen enough devils. You don't want to see any more. Remember the night you came into my cell and went on your knees and asked me to forgive you? What did you

82

say that night? You gave me your gun and asked me to shoot you. Eh? What did I say? Eh?'

McDara furiously caught Fetch by the chest and shook him violently.

'Lemme go, damn you!' growled Fetch.

McDara loosed his hold, leaned closer and continued:

'I told you I had a job for you, didn't I? Well, this is it. And don't you forget, Gutty, you're going through with it, the way I say, or . . .'

The car stopped. The two men started and remained motionless until the bell tinkled again. The car hurtled forward.

'What did ye say?' said Fetch.

McDara grinned and said, nodding his head:

'She knows.'

Fetch started and said in a hoarse voice, through his trembling lips:

'Who does?'

'She does. Kitty Mellett. Go on. You can strangle me or plug me here now, but they'll get you, old son.'

Fetch became lax.

'I got him with that lie,' thought McDara. 'He won't start again.'

'Well!' he said aloud. 'Are you going through with it?'

'You're a devil,' panted Fetch. 'I'll do it, but I'll get you yet. Afterwards. Savvy? Hey! Why the hell didn't ye leave me alone? I was all right in New

York. I had forgotten all about this cursed country.
Why didn't ye leave me where I was?'

McDara got to his feet, put his hands in his raincoat pockets, leaned forward and whispered:

'Lie low, old son. You won't have long to wait.
I'll see to that.'

He walked away. Fetch called after him:

'Where are ye goin'?'

McDara turned back. Fetch had got to his feet to
follow him.

'You stay where you are,' he said sharply. 'Be at
home to-night about eleven o'clock. I'll come and
tell you what's to be done after I see Tumulty.'

Fetch slouched back on to his seat. McDara got
off the tram-car at the next stop. He stood on the
pavement looking after the retreating car. He saw
Fetch up there, crouching over the wire rails, looking
out upon the river, with his jaw in his palm. McDara
grinned again. He felt possessed of terrible power.
All his fears vanished. He became terribly calm and
as solid as a ball of metal. He moved away. As he
walked, he felt his thighs were made of iron.

He had descended near Capel Street. He walked
up that street in order to reconnoitre the spot where
he was to meet Kitty Mellett at eight o'clock. He
reached the spot and stood there looking about him.

It was at the corner of a narrow lane leading from
Capel Street into the Smithfield Market. The lane
was full of open-air shops, owned by Jewish mer-
chants. It was packed with people and with goods

exposed for sale, hanging carpets, beds, crockery and ready-made clothes. The lane was choked up and there was a smell of dust.

'It's a good place,' he thought. 'Very quiet.'

Then, as he stood there, a shiver passed down his spine. For the first time, HE, who was doomed to die, stood out before his mind in his physical shape, with his long nose, his razor lips and his cruel, greedy eyes.

With a queer, animal movement, he turned his head to one side and looked into the distance, with his upper lip twisted in a snarl. There was an expression of hopeless despair in his sunken eyes.

Then he moved off, slouching, with stooping shoulders, to his lodgings.

CHAPTER SEVEN

At eight o'clock McDara came again to the appointed place. It was raining heavily. He took shelter in the closed doorway of a shop at the corner of the lane. The street was empty on account of the heavy downpour. Here and there, in other doorways, there were human figures. A stray person dashed along, stooping forward. The street lights were blurred. The innumerable drops of rain, falling on the smooth roadway, made a soft, hissing sound. Big blobs of water splashed from the roofs of houses on to the pavement. In the distance, there was the rattle of tram-cars and the hoot-hoot of motors; as if terrified by the heavy rain.

The street had become a dark tunnel, wrapped in subtle gloom, with a lightless sky above and dark, dripping house walls on either side. He stared into the roadway, rigid, without thought. Now he was indifferent to her approach. The torture of anxiety had passed. The idea in his mind had reached maturity, absorbing his whole being. Now his mind was a hard substance impervious to fear. His imagination had frozen up. His muscles were fixed. He had become colour blind. Everything was black. Now there was no NEED to think, or to fear that ANYTHING could prevent the iron ball in his brain from reaching its destination in the brain of its objective. He had begun to experience the furious ecstasy of assassination.

In this state, he felt possessed of such power that he had merely to will a thing and it should be done.

Although many minutes passed after the hour had struck, he did not look up. His ears were lax. He stood there like a ghoul in the dark doorway, with his shabby cap aslant over his left eye, with the other eye, sunken and fixed, looking into the roadway, with stooping shoulders, with his shapeless, long raincoat hanging like a shroud about him.

Then suddenly she appeared from the laneway on the left. She lowered her umbrella and entered the doorway beside him. He shivered slightly but he did not speak or look at her. His sunken eye still remained fixed on the roadway.

'Hello, Mac,' she whispered.

'Hello,' he murmured. 'Get him?'

'Yes,' she said.

'Right. Where is he?'

She shook the rain off her umbrella and then unhitched the clasp. It fell slack. She went in farther until she was nearly behind him. She whispered the name of a street and asked him did he know it. He growled and nodded his head.

'What number?' he said.

'The number is no use,' she said. 'There are no numbers on some of the doors. It's right opposite a little huckster's shop. The door is open and you'll see a man there in the doorway wearing a brown overcoat. It's not far if you go . . .'

'All right. I know it. Listen.'

'What?'

'You didn't tell him anything, did you?'

'No.'

'All right. Did you do anything about the other business?'

'Yes. A little. It might take a little time. But I'll do my best to get it as soon as possible.'

'Be very careful. As soon as you find out anything definite, report to me at my room. I'll wait in, every evening at seven o'clock. Come dressed as you were before. Remember that. I'll give out to the landlady that you are a representative of the British Legion. A welfare worker or something like that. Be very careful.'

'Leave it to me, Mac.'

'Have no truck with your own crowd. Go on your own . . . among the people I told you about. Be casual, you see. A chance word, if you can draw it . . . that's the best way. Don't hustle them.'

'Yes, yes. I'm not a child.'

'Still . . . good luck, Kitty. You had better move on now.'

Suddenly he realized that he was speaking very gruffly. The same instinct, that had made him glance amorously at his landlady, now made him put back his hand and grip Kitty by the arm. He felt her start. He moved his arm and put it around her waist. She began to tremble. He could hear her breathe. His body became passionate. But, unseen in the darkness, his sunken eyes glittered. His face wrinkled

with silent laughter. Then he heard her say, gasping:
'For God's sake, Michael!' He took away his arm.

As she went past him, going out, their faces were
close. He saw a gleaming light in her eyes. Neither
spoke. She walked away. He stared into the roadway again.

'That is very strange,' he muttered.

Suddenly a faint thought entered his mind, as from
a great distance. It tottered there for a few moments
and he saw a place of abandoned revelry. He nodded
his head. The tiny thought vanished. Then he
coughed, shrugged himself, stamped his feet and set
out from the doorway at a fast pace, going northwards.

After walking for ten minutes through slum
streets, he came to a short road of tenement houses.
He saw the little huckster's shop. He went up to
the window and pretended to examine the articles for
sale. Then he turned around casually and glanced at
the opposite side of the street. There were tall, dis-
reputable houses on that side. Most of the doors
stood ajar. One door was wide open. As he looked,
a man wearing an overcoat came forward to the thres-
hold and glanced up and down the street. McDara
went into the shop and bought a packet of cigarettes.
He came out and walked across the street to the open
door. He walked up the steps slowly until he reached
the man.

'Is that you, Frank?' he said in a low voice.

'Is it Mac?' said the other man.

McDara nodded. They went into the dark hall. They clasped hands. The man was Francis Tumulty.

'Come on upstairs,' he whispered. 'I have a room here. I thought you had better come here as your friend said you were on the dodge. It's safe here. Mind the steps.'

They went up several flights of stairs to the top floor. It grew darker as they ascended. Tumulty kept striking matches. The banisters were torn in places. There were holes in the stairs. There was a dank smell of laundry and of babies. Gleams of light came from the uneven bottoms of doors as they passed. They heard voices. One voice in particular, that of a powerful man, kept repeating drunkenly: 'Twenty to one. God's curse. And I had only a bob on each way.'

On the top floor, Tumulty unlocked a door and led McDara into a room. Then he locked the door on the inside. It was pitch-dark. He struck a match.

'I wasn't sure you'd come,' he said, 'so I didn't light the fire. It's set, though.'

He lit a paraffin lamp that hung on a nail in the wall. He took off his overcoat and threw it on a chair. McDara began to unbutton his wet raincoat.

'Sit down,' said Tumulty, 'until I get the fire lit.'

McDara hung his coat on the back of the door. He looked around the room, sniffing. There was a heavy smell, as if the room were usually shut up and unventilated. There was a double bed, a few chairs and a washstand. That was all. He took one of the chairs to the front of the fire and sat down. Tumulty put an old newspaper against an upstanding poker in front of the lighted fire. Then he stood up. He put his hands on his hips and looked at McDara.

He was a powerfully built man, nearly six feet in height, with a massive chest. His biceps bulged through his coat sleeves. His neck was short and thick. His head was square, with powerful jaws and a full forehead. His face was bronzed and rather fat. His eyes were small. They had that expression of aggressive self-confidence which is only seen in the eyes of strong, athletic men, who are devoid of imagination. His lips were greedy and rather sensual. He stood like a soldier on parade, with rigid thighs.

He was already a little beyond the prime of youth, although he was only thirty-one years of age. He had a very slight paunch and his limbs were becoming fleshy. But this slight deterioration had not yet begun to impair his vitality and strength. He seemed to be made of iron, solid, full of power.

'God!' he said in a low, tense voice, that was strangely musical coming from such a heavy man. 'It's good to see you again, Mac. Where have you been? You look as if you had a tough time of it. You changed a lot. I hardly recognize you, man.'

'That so?' said McDara, looking up. 'You got fat, Frank.'

Tumulty laughed boisterously and stroked his stomach.

'They say the Corporation is disbanded,' he said, 'but mine is expanding.'

He laughed again at his crude joke. McDara did not even smile.

'Is it quite safe here, Frank?' he said. 'Who else lives on this floor?'

'Only a tart,' said Tumulty. 'She's out . . . going her rounds.'

'I see,' said McDara.

McDara spoke in a gloomy, hard voice. Tumulty suddenly lost his boisterous mood and his face became serious. He brought up another chair and sat down beside McDara. They were silent a little while.

'Well!' said McDara at length. 'You were surprised to hear I was in town. What?'

'I could hardly believe it. I thought you were gone under or something.'

'I bet. I suppose you heard the rumours?'

'Yes.'

'Did you believe them?'

'No.'

'Good lad, Frank. I put them out myself. I've been lying low for a certain purpose.'

They became silent again. They lit cigarettes.

'Why the name o' God didn't ye drop us a line?' said Tumulty.

'Didn't know your address,' said McDara. 'And I was taking no chances with a messenger. I cut adrift entirely.'

'Did you stay in the United States?'

'No. I went all round. I've been around the world.'

'I see.'

They became silent again.

'Are you long back?' Tumulty said.

'A few days.'

'Are you staying long?'

McDara paused. Then he looked at Tumulty and said:

'That depends on you.'

Again they smoked in silence.

'Do you live here?' McDara said.

'No,' said Tumulty. 'I use it for a certain purpose.'

'I see,' said McDara. 'Still active?'

Tumulty pursed up his lips and nodded his head. The two men looked closely at one another.

'I cut out on my own too,' said Tumulty.

'I know,' murmured McDara. 'I remember the last time I was talking to you, you had a plan. That's over three years ago now. Do you remember? Boxing Day, I think it was. In camp.'

'Yes. You were in an awful state then, Mac. I thought you were out of your mind.'

'H'm! I made a plan of my own that time too.'

'Ha, ha! I remember your mother died about that time, didn't she?'

'I remember your proposition. I was often wondering how you got on. That's principally why I dug you up.'

Tumulty leaned forward.

'Are you going to muck in with me now?' he said.

McDara shook his head.

'No, but I want you to muck in with me, though,' he said.

Tumulty threw his cigarette-end into the fire and rubbed his large, muscular hands together. McDara watched him. Tumulty took off his hat and threw it on the floor. He was slightly bald over his forehead. His fair hair was cropped very closely. One ear stuck out more than the other. In his bare head, he looked rather like a prize-fighter.

'What's the game?' he said, looking into the fire.

'Well! That's what I want to discuss with you. But, first of all . . . have you really cut adrift? Are you still connected with the volunteers?'

'No. They expelled me.'

'What for?'

Tumulty made a gesture of contempt and said slowly:

'Dis-rup-tion. A damn lot of . . . I wanted to get something done in England. There was a big chance there last year during the general strike. We could have crippled the country. Crease one or two of the labour fellows. Then double up on a couple of the capitalist crowd. Then put up a few plants. Ye'd have civil war in no time.'

'I see,' said McDara. 'The Executive wouldn't touch it.'

'No damn fear.'

94

McDara smiled faintly and said:

'Why didn't you go ahead on your own? You should have a few men together by now.'

Tumulty turned towards McDara and held out his hand. He slowly brushed his thumb against the first and second fingers.

'Money,' he said. 'That and the fact that I have only key men. Ye'd want, in a foreign country, a covering organization for the couple of men required for the job.'

'I know,' said McDara. 'You're wrong, though, Frank.'

'How d'ye mean?' said Tumulty sharply.

'Charity begins at home,' said McDara in a harsh whisper.

Tumulty's little eyes glistened. He opened his lips and then slowly drew the lower lip downwards over the upper lip. He did not reply, but he looked at McDara's thin legs with great interest.

'It would be all right starting something in England if that country were ripe for revolution,' said McDara, 'or if we were ready to avail of an opportunity in England. But neither case is . . . Tchee! Food for only one man out of . . . If you struck at them, they'd all turn on you, both the labour crowd and the capitalist crowd.'

'I don't know about that,' said Tumulty. 'I believe there's a lot in this Communist business, if we could work it right, in England and in Ulster. Then walk in.'

'I know, I know,' said McDara irritably. 'If we could get to the moon there's possibly a lot of gold there. But where's the IDEA behind your plan?'

'How do you mean?' said Tumulty. 'The overthrow of the enemy. That's idea enough.'

McDara looked at him coldly.

'You can't succeed without a religious idea,' he said. 'We have no religion.'

'You mean the priests are against us.'

McDara threw his cigarette-end into the fire.

'You know,' he said, 'there's no revolutionary movement in this country.'

Tumulty made another sneering gesture.

'That's well known,' he said.

'I mean,' said McDara, 'we have advanced to a certain point and then . . . then thought is necessary. We have advanced so far without thought. Now, though, from this onwards, thought is necessary.'

Tumulty's eyes began to grow suspicious.

'Come on, Mac,' he said. 'Let up on it.'

'Wait a moment,' said McDara. 'I've got a proposition to make to you. I want to explain first the idea behind my . . . my . . . what I'm going to DO.'

'Go ahead,' said Tumulty, spitting into the fire. 'I'm listening.'

'Well!' said McDara. 'In the first place, our business is not to cripple England but to create a superior type of human being here. That is the objective of the revolutionary, to create a superior type of human being. Most revolutionary movements make the

96

mistake of aiming at a change of government, seizing political power and that sort of thing. That is not revolution. It is merely a transposition of the material wealth in a community.'

Tumulty contracted his eyebrows. His underlip closed over his upper lip, in a gesture of violent contempt. McDara paused and then continued gloomily:

'Power should always be in the hands of inferior types, because power has a demoralizing influence. When a strong man seizes power, he should be cut down at once. Because the mass feels inferior to a strong man. Each individual loses his initiative. The strong man sucks all power into his own being. The mass become slaves. No progress is made. Until the head is chopped off. Then the mass is free to grope about again. Each individual becomes a living force, groping forward, unimpeded. Do you see?'

Tumulty rubbed his large palms, one against the other, slowly. He opened his lips and looked at McDara suspiciously. Then he shook his head.

'Listen,' said McDara excitedly. 'There are never more than a handful of revolutionary minds in any country. They therefore must stand apart and make no attempt to direct the Government, actually. If they take part in the administration of the Government, they either become tyrants because they are strong, or corrupt because they desire money or sensuality. They must live like hermits and strike

97

down whatever individual tries to arrest the progress of the community. There is only one way to do that.'

He paused and looked at Tumulty. His eyes glittered. Tumulty suddenly sat erect and put his closed fists on his widespread knees.

'What way is that?' he said.

McDara whispered, almost inaudibly, with a sibilant sound:

'Assassination.'

Very slowly, Tumulty leaned forward until his elbows reached his knees. Then again he rubbed his large palms together.

'Eh?' said McDara in a querulous tone.

McDara was shivering spasmodically. His sunken eyes glittered brilliantly. Tumulty nodded his head and whispered:

'Now I see what you were driving at.'

Then he sat erect and said fiercely:

'I know the man you're driving at too.'

McDara's eyes became cold.

'That so?' he said.

Then they became silent, looking at one another. But although their lips were silent, their eyes spoke. In such moments, eyes read thoughts.

'Well!' said McDara. 'Do you agree?'

'So that was your plan?' said Tumulty.

'Yes,' said McDara.

'Ever since . . . for three years . . . you've been . . .'

'Yes . . . ever since, I've been working it out.'

'Supposing somebody else had . . .'

'I knew nobody would have.'

'Why?'

'Because nobody had the IDEA.'

'Eh?'

Tumulty started. For the first time, an expression of respect came into his self-confident, strong man's eyes. He examined McDara's emaciated face that was now glowing with exaltation. Then a feeling of jealousy made him become antagonistic; as if attempting to make a last effort to maintain his sense of superiority.

'You think so,' he said. 'I often thought of it, though. So did others. Not only among our fellows but among his own crowd.'

'Yes,' said McDara viciously. 'But nobody *did* it. Eh?'

'Matter of policy,' said Tumulty.

'That be damned,' said McDara. 'It is always good policy to pull a weed. Nobody had the IDEA. That's why. Without an idea behind it, every political act becomes immoral and unnecessary. Such an act as this should be done in cold blood, not for motives of revenge or greed or for the purpose of seizing power or for anything else. Merely to cut off the head that is blocking the forward movement of the mass. Listen. You remember, during the years we fought the English, we had no head. Each worked on his own account, almost, at least in small

99

groups. We progressed. We produced fine types of individuals. We almost freed ourselves from superstition. I had almost forgotten that, Frank. This act must also be directed against the idea of God.'

Tumulty's lips began to move, as if to make a statement, but he said nothing. He began instead to snap the joints of his fingers. McDara watched him. Then McDara said:

'I want to make everything clear before we discuss the matter. Otherwise . . .'

'Otherwise what?' said Tumulty.

'It would be no use,' said McDara. 'Our people must make a great gesture of defiance before they can free themselves. They must trample on everything. On God too.'

Tumulty sighed heavily. Then he said:

'Listen, Mac. Are you just talking, or do you mean business?'

'I mean business.'

'You do?'

'Yes,' said McDara, with great fervour.

'Well,' said Tumulty, 'if you can put forward a plan that's likely to . . .'

'Be quite confident about that,' said McDara. 'I've got a plan and the necessary funds to carry it through. I mean enough to provide a getaway. Not that I give tuppence about my life, but it's necessary that it should be a mystery in order to have full effect.'

'Now you're talking,' said Tumulty eagerly. 'Let's

have a deck at your idea. One moment, though. What about your friend?'

'Kitty Mellett?'

'Did you tell her anything?'

'Yes. She's in with me to a certain point.'

Tumulty's face grew dark.

'Don't worry, Frank,' said McDara. 'She's steel. I know her of old. And there's a reason for her inclusion which I'll explain. Do you agree to come in with me?'

Tumulty paused for a long time, looking into the fire, snapping his finger joints. McDara waited trembling. Tumulty rose to his feet and folded his arms. He looked into the fire, with his back turned towards McDara. McDara rose to his feet, crouching like an animal ready to spring on his prey. His eyes were fixed on the centre of Tumulty's back. He held his hands in front of his chest with the fingers laced in an attitude of prayer. He held his breath. His body was rigid. His face assumed an expression of violent concentration. He gritted his teeth. Every atom of his energy was drawing Tumulty towards him, forcing him to turn around and bow down before him.

Tumulty's back quivered. His left shoulder rose up slowly and then, with a sudden movement, he brought his left arm sharply to his side, close against his heart.

McDara's face broke into a silent grin. Then it became rigid again.

Tumulty turned around suddenly. His fleshy cheeks were pale.

'All right,' he whispered through clenched teeth. 'Remember, though, I never turn back once I start a thing, and . . . I have ten men. We are all oath-bound. An injury to one . . .'

With his left hand, McDara wrenched back his coat and waistcoat, exposing his shirt, over the region of his heart.

'See,' he said. 'Whenever you think fit. Fire. Only . . . Let it be done first. Let it be DONE. I'll lead myself.'

Tumulty quivered from head to foot. His thick neck became florid. Then he said:

'I trust you, Mac. How many men will we want?'

'One more,' said McDara.

'Then, sit down and let's talk it over.'

They sat down side by side.

CHAPTER EIGHT

AFTER leaving McDara, Kitty Mellett went to the Shelbourne Hotel. She entered the lounge and took a chair just within the door, near the fire in the ante-room. She was in a position to see and be seen by every one that entered or left the lounge. She ordered coffee, settled herself comfortably in her chair and began to watch the door of the dining-room across the hall.

She was waiting for a certain man, whom she knew to be having dinner in the dining-room.

Her heart was beating loudly. Until now she had been calm and almost unaware of what she was help-ing McDara to do. Now, however, she had been touched by him. It seemed that his touch had awakened her to the reality of his purpose. His touch had awakened in her being something that was acting like a drug, heaving up in waves, exciting her. She kept wrinkling her forehead as if looking at something strange. There were voices in her ears. She understood what was going to be done, no longer in relation to herself, but in relation to society. She felt that the eyes of the whole community were fixed on her.

She felt that she was in McDara's power and that, if he touched her again, or looked at her with his sunken eyes, she would shriek and fall down dead. She must obey his will. But the countless eyes of the people were gazing at her in warning, telling her not to obey his will. She kept repeating to herself hysterically that she must obey.

'It is a holy act, a holy act,' she thought. 'The dead cry out for vengeance. Ireland in chains. . . .'

The waiter brought her coffee. She sipped a little. Then she felt better. She noticed that her hand was trembling while it held the cup. She had put down the cup, though, before she noticed that her hand had trembled while holding it. Her mind took a long time to receive impressions. This trivial discovery changed the direction of her excitement. She became violently angry.

First she became angry with the back of the departing waiter. The slave! He crawled away like a worm, a fine, strong man, dressed up like an ape, bowing and scraping, instead of being a soldier with a gun on his shoulder.

'What are all these people doing here?' she thought. 'The parasites! The slaves! Why don't they rise up and fight against slavery?'

She looked back into the lounge. She saw an enormously fat woman, with bare neck and shoulders, reclining in an arm-chair. The woman had jewels on her fat neck and on her flabby hands. Her feet were propped up on a cushion. She had a heavy jowl. She looked unhappy, suffering either from sore feet or indigestion; goodness knows from what she suffered. But Kitty did not pity her suffering face. To Kitty she was symbolical of the degradation of the people, sin and gluttony and acceptance of tyranny. A parasite! Something to be torn limb from limb, to be wiped out, to be burned alive.

A picture of the starving people came before Kitty's mind and she saw them pouring into this hotel, after the act, with axes and sledge-hammers. . . .

A half-hour passed.

'I can't sit here any longer,' she thought. 'Why didn't he let me work the usual channels? Why all this mystery? Why not rise out and slay him publicly and call on the people to rise . . . ?'

Suddenly she started. She looked towards the door. Like magic, the worried, angry look left her countenance. Her face assumed an amorous, coquet-tish look. Four men were approaching from the dining-room. They were apparently slightly intoxi-cated. They were laughing and talking loudly. A large man with an enormous stomach walked in front. He had heavy, florid cheeks. On his left there was a tall, thin man with grey hair. On his right there was a dark man with a thick underlip. A little distance to the rear there was a handsome, young man, frowning and looking at the ground. This young man walked with the exaggerated dignity of intoxication.

Kitty smiled at the leader of the party. He stood still when he saw her. He touched the arm of the man on his left. Then, with a buffoonish gesture, he raised his hands slightly above his head, in an attitude of surrender.

'Peace or war?' he said.

Then he burst out laughing. His enormous stomach and his brick-red, heavy cheeks shook with laughter. But although his body made violent efforts to utter a thunderous peal of laughter, the result of its efforts, in sound, was incredibly small. A faint squeak issued from his purple lips. In his voluminous throat there was a hoarse gurgle. It seemed that his throat was blocked up and that violent peals of laughter were pushed back into his enormous stomach, where they heaved about, straining against its distended walls.

This man was Mr. Timothy McShiel, T.D., a member of the Government party. He was fifty-five years old, as bald as an egg, short in stature, with diminutive feet, large hands and cunning blue eyes. Although he was a prominent member of the Government party, the Executive were in doubt about his fidelity; and justly so. For Mr. McShiel was a typical politician of the old school. Like the gentleman in Joyce's *Ulysses*, he was always in doubt whether he should raise his hat to the Lord-Lieutenant or pass by without saluting. He was always trying to sit on the fence, waiting to jump in on the side of the winning team. Thus, he intrigued with the Republicans in secret, and within his own party he formed caucuses for the purpose of blackmailing the Executive. At the same time, in private, he gave the Imperialist element to understand that he was at heart an Imperialist and was only restrained from coming out openly with a Union Jack in his button-hole by the fact that such conduct would only result in his downfall and in putting an extremist in his place. He always managed to surround himself with such a web of intrigue and cunning plans that he himself never knew exactly where he was or what party he was supporting at the moment. In spite of that, he was very popular. He had all the genial qualities of the old generation, that is now being swallowed up by the dour puritanism of the young generation, arisen since the revolution. He was hospitable, generous, brimful of funny stories, with all the mannerisms of the charming buffoon. Therefore, although every one knew that he went back on his word, betrayed his friends, took bribes and was as slippery as an eel, he was received everywhere socially, he was sought after by clerics for public functions, and the Executive found him useful for the purpose of intriguing with pliable members of the opposition.

Mr. McShiel owned two public-houses and three farms. He could read and write fairly well. He bred hunters and owned a couple of race-horses. He had become rich since the establishment of the new Government, by manipulating the first-hand knowledge he received of budgets, of new companies that were being subsidized and of industries that were going to be protected. He had surrounded himself with a whole army of relatives and friends, for whom he had secured Government positions. He was an ardent Catholic. When he was drunk, which happened very frequently, he shed tears of love for Ireland, whom he called, affectionately, 'the little brown bog.'

'Here she is,' he said to his friends in a humorous voice. 'An old friend who disapproves of my character. We are all traitors, so beware. Beware of the angry gleam in the eyes of Kathleen O'Hooligan.'

His friends had become serious. They only smiled faintly at this sally. They all knew Kitty Mellett and considered her a 'notorious character.' Two of them, furthermore, felt ashamed in her presence, because they had begun their careers as Republicans and had got into their present positions by forswearing their political beliefs.

These two were the man with the thick underlip and the young man who walked in the rear. The man with the thick underlip was a Labour leader called Tynum. The young man in the rear was an official called Carmody.

The third man was called Jenkins. He was a rich man, a capitalist and an Imperialist. He assumed a bored, severe expression. He was not ashamed in Kitty's presence. On the contrary, he disliked and despised her for being a rebel. He also despised the company he was with and considered that the buffoonish conduct of McShiel was 'going a little too far.'

Tynum, the Labour leader, looked about him suspiciously, thinking:

'Now, this devil has seen me here with Jenkins and McShiel. It'll be all over town to-morrow that I was seen drunk at the Shelbourne Hotel, smokin' cigars, wastin' the workers' money and bein' bought by the Government and the Freemasons. Of course they'll add that I was with a flash tart and went off in a motor to the flats. Holy God!'

He trembled with fright, thinking of a recent *coup* by the police, when a certain prominent man was caught naked in bed with a woman in a brothel.

Carmody was even more affected by seeing Kitty. He straightened himself, flushed and began to tremble. Then his face clouded with anger.

'Well!' said Kitty to McShiel. 'I'm glad to see you are enjoying yourself. Have a good time?'

Jenkins touched McShiel's arm, in an effort to get him to move on. But at that moment Kitty pushed aside her coat and leaned farther back in her chair, showing her graceful and attractive figure. McShiel's eyes immediately saw 'her points.' He brushed away Jenkins' arm irritably.

'Begob, Kitty,' he said in a low voice. 'If ye were a filly I'd buy ye.'

Then he laughed. Kitty, with a pretence at being slightly offended, blushed and wrapped her coat about her.

'Come an' have a liqueur with us,' said McShiel. 'We are all Irish, no matter how . . . come on. Madame, give me your arm.'

Kitty resisted for a little while and then got to her feet. McShiel led her up the lounge, looking about him with a laughing face, as much as to say: 'See what a tartar I've got. I'm the boy for 'em.'

They sat down at a table at the far end of the lounge. McShiel ordered liqueurs. Then he began to talk. He cracked jokes and told funny stories, in order to restore the good spirits of the company. He passed around cigarettes, spoke to everybody in turn, introduced Kitty several times to each of his friends, bantered, laughed, cajoled, poked Jenkins in the ribs and forced everybody by sheer persistence to laugh with him. At that moment it was impossible to believe that the man was a mountebank or a scoundrel. In his company, everything assumed a different value. Religion, morals, ideals all floated away and assumed grotesque characters. Nothing seemed real or worth-while but laughter, merry scheming and mockery.

After all . . . What is good?

Even Tynum, with his dark, suspicious face and his thick underlip, began to laugh. He turned towards Kitty and said in a pompous voice:

'I'll tell you about a funny request I got from one of your people yesterday.'

'What do you mean by one of my people?' said Kitty contemptuously.

She had nothing to gain from the Labour leader, so she felt she could show her contempt for him openly. For she knew that the other members of the company despised him and were only using him for political reasons.

McShiel, scenting a quarrel, leaned across the table and said, with a chuckle:

'Are ye still carrying bombs, Kitty?'

'Do you know, Tim,' said Kitty with a smile, 'I used to believe in you once.'

'That's bad,' said McShiel. 'Never believe in anything 'till it's past the post and its number is hoisted.'

Then he laughed again. He was delighted that Kitty was treating him as a friend. He still had a sentimental respect for those who had remained faithful to the Republican cause. And his natural shrewdness suggested to him that it was just as well to keep friendly with the Republicans. One never knew but there might be another revolution on the morrow, placing the Republicans in power. Mr. McShiel calculated on being just as indispensable to the Republicans, should they overthrow the present Government, as he was to the present Government that had conquered the Republicans.

Tynum, the Labour leader, turned to Jenkins, the capitalist, and whispered:

'They abuse us in public and then they come to us in private, on their knees, asking us to petition the Government for this prisoner and that prisoner.'

The sleeve of Jenkins' dinner-jacket shivered slightly. It had come in contact with the rough tweed on Tynum's elbow. Jenkins sniffed and said coldly:

'Indeed! How curious!'

'Kitty,' said McShiel, 'yer a foolish girl. Why don't ye settle down and have sense? What we want is unity.'

He struck the table.

'Unity,' he said, looking around the table. 'A united Ireland could conquer the world. Give an' take. Eh? Gentlemen!'

Unity was always McShiel's programme, because it did not necessitate taking sides on any definite question. It led nowhere because all the other politicians, whom he proposed to unite under one banner, were like himself; with the only difference that some were less clever. As it was impossible to impose a budget on the community sufficiently large to provide emoluments for all the politicians simultaneously, it was obviously impossible to unite them. But the programme was attractive, as it allowed of unlimited intrigue.

'Little gatherings like this,' he said, stretching out his hands, 'can do more than bullets. All classes and opinions, with the one common denominator, whom we all love in our own tin-pot way. The little brown bog. Then, sir, it's a case of the rest nowhere and we win with the jockey sittin' on her.'

'Talking about horses,' began Jenkins coldly, 'I have a good tip.'

Carmody, the young official, had until now been sitting in silence beside Kitty, with his hands clasped between his crossed knees. Looking very smart in a well-cut dinner-jacket, with a stern, intellectual face, he had been gazing in a melancholy fashion at the table as if immersed in a deep problem of State. There was something curiously clean and moral and dignified about his countenance. And yet, in his eyes, there was a suggestion of a spiritual cloud which he could not dispel. Ambition?

Now, however, when the other three men began to discuss horses, he turned towards Kitty and said with great force:

'What we need is the iron heel in this country.'

Kitty looked at him sweetly, rubbing the back of her right hand with the fingers of her left hand. She said, with a faint smile:

'It's a long time since I've seen you, Tom.'

'Yes,' said Carmody, 'the iron heel.'

He frowned and looked at the table.

'I hear you have a new job, Tom,' said Kitty. 'You're in the Ministry of Justice now, aren't you?'

'It's very complimentary to feel that I'm still of interest to your intelligence staff,' said Carmody, speaking with the slow pompous manner of an intoxicated person.

'Perhaps you are making a mistake,' said Kitty. 'You're taking a lot for granted.'

'How do you mean?' said Carmody, looking up.

Kitty laughed.

'You think,' she said, 'because you were an officer in the Free State army during the Civil War and arrested me once that I still take the trouble to hate you and that our intelligence staff, as you say, take note of your movements. Don't flatter yourself, Tom. You're not worth the trouble. I think you're just weak. In a way, I pity you.'

Carmody flushed angrily.

'However,' continued Kitty, 'it's good to hear you talk of the iron heel. Your heel, is it? There's only one man in the Government who has enough brains to use the iron heel, and he is a coward. The iron heel needs courage. REAL courage.'

Carmody leaned towards her and said:

'Ha! You're afraid of him, aren't you? And . . . he's not a coward. He's fearless. You hate him because he beat you to a standstill. You people have an inferiority complex. You love to be down-trodden. You hate to be deprived of the right to whinge and cry about your sufferings. When a man rises up and tries to hammer our people into shape, to mould the country into self-respect, to discipline a nation of slaves . . . eh . . . ruthless government. . . . Eh? You . . . you stab him in the back. That's how it is. We need the iron heel and . . . By God! we'll have it too. He's going to give it to you.'

'You're getting excited, Tom,' said Kitty softly. 'You've been drinking too much.'

Carmody scowled, took up his glass and drained it, as if to show her that he could drink still more without being affected by it.

'Whenever I hear of a man being ruthless,' said

Kitty, 'I always suspect he is a coward. Do you remember the Tsar of Russia that shot his secretary because he put his hand in his pocket? That's the way with our strong man. He goes about guarded by a crowd of thugs.'

'That's a lie,' said Carmody hotly.

'Tell that to the Marines,' said Kitty. 'They sleep under his bed at night and go to the altar-rails with him on Sundays.'

'That's a damn lie,' said Carmody. 'I go to Mass to the same Church myself every Sunday. The same Mass too. He never has a guard. I've seen him come from his house absolutely alone and . . .'

'Now, what's the big argument?' said McShiel.

'Tom was saying that we need strong government,' said Kitty.

'I quite agree,' said Jenkins.

'Yes,' said McShiel. 'Unity, thy name is strength.'

'That horse,' said Tynum to McShiel, ''ll never do three miles over that heavy country with that weight on his back. He'll come down at the water.'

The three men resumed the argument over horses.

'On State occasions,' continued Carmody. 'I grant you that. But to Mass . . . never. NEVER. It's just mean, spiteful jealousy that makes Republicans put out these stories. They are beaten. They can no longer do any harm. So they sneer. That's all. They are just forcing the Government into the hands of the enemy. I'm a Republican. A better Republican than you are.'

'That so?' said Kitty.

'Yes,' said Carmody, 'that's so. I support the language, Irish games, Irish manufactures. I'm helping to build up the country. That's Republicanism. That's nationalism. You people are anarchists.'

Kitty was no longer listening to him.

'I must make sure,' she thought. 'I must get him out of here.'

Carmody rambled on, talking with great vehemence.

Suddenly, Kitty sighed, dropped her head and said wearily:

'Maybe you're right, Tom. But how are we to do anything when we're never given a chance?'

'How do you mean?' said Carmody.

'You're bitter against us.'

'Oh! No,' said Carmody. 'I'm not bitter. But why don't you chuck it?'

'How do you know I haven't chucked it?'

Carmody opened his eyes and said:

'Have you, though?'

Kitty looked away and whispered:

'Oh, don't nag at me. I'm fed up.'

'Sorry,' said Carmody.

Kitty took out her handkerchief.

After a pause she looked up at him with a tearful face and said:

'Have you got your car here?'

'Yes,' he said, flushing slightly.

'Would you drive me home?' she said. 'I don't feel very well.'

They excused themselves and left the hotel together.

CHAPTER NINE

JUST when Kitty Mellett was leaving the hotel with Carmody, McDara began to unfold his plan to Tumulty.

He pulled his chair close up to the fire and held out his left hand to the flames, with the palm upwards. Then he began to draw figures on his left palm with his right forefinger as he spoke. As soon as he began to speak, his face became exalted. His eyes darted from his palm to Tumulty's face and back again. He spoke in a hushed whisper, with great passion. It was obvious that every word was precious to him; as if he had wrought each word, through long nights of agony, forging the plan.

Now his emaciated body no longer looked paltry. He was possessed by such enthusiasm, like a creative frenzy, that his face shone, casting a glamour over his whole frame, enlarging him, giving him the stature of a giant.

Tumulty listened with open lips. Now and again, he lisped: 'Yes. I see.' His eyes were distended. Every time that McDara looked at him, he felt afraid, as in the presence of something occult. Little by little his brain became overwrought, listening. The words grew terrifying. He ceased to understand them. He furrowed his forehead and looked towards the window. There was a tall steeple silhouetted against the dark sky, afar off. A tall, thin blur.

His mouth opened wide and he thought how pleasant it was, after all, to be an insurance agent, wandering around, collecting money during the week, canvassing . . . and then on Saturdays to go away somewhere with the fellows on the spree . . . a girl maybe . . . bring one up here sometime . . . his band of ten men . . . why not put up a bank instead and beat it with a load of money?

He began to tremble, contemplating the pleasure of having a woman's soft breasts against his body.

McDara noticed him trembling. McDara's eyes gleamed. He paused for a moment, smiled faintly and continued. Tumulty frowned, closed his mouth, threw up his chin and laced his fingers in front of his chest.

'Yes,' he whispered, through his teeth. 'I see.'

McDara finished and leaned back, with his palms on his knees.

'You see,' he said eagerly. 'I think I have it as tight as a drum. Do you find any flaw in it?'

Tumulty drew in a deep breath and raised his eyebrows. Then he began slowly to ask questions, almost in a timid voice.

'Why three cars?' he said.

'Why?' said McDara. 'That's obvious. Pick one, change the number, then they won't know which car. We need one, but we must pinch three at least.'

'How about . . . ?'

Tumulty began to ask innumerable questions. McDara answered each slowly, gradually becoming

angry in his replies. He was as jealous of criticism as
an artist who had spent years creating a masterpiece.

At last, however, he noticed a certain quality in
Tumulty's voice that made him start. He leaned
forward, caught Tumulty by the chest and looked
upwards into his face.

'D'ye want to pull out, Frank?' he said in a low
voice.

Tumulty sat erect like a bolt and caressed his
upper lip with his lower lip.

'Hold on now,' he said, through his teeth. 'Don't
rush things.'

'Blast him,' thought McDara, 'I'll have to rush
him. He has no guts after all.'

'Don't rush things,' repeated Tumulty. 'You
haven't said who the other man is going to be yet.
Who's going to drive the car? I can't drive very well.
We'd have to have a crackerjack of a driver for a job
like this.'

'I've got the man,' asid McDara quietly. 'I
brought him over from New York. He can do anything with a car short of making it fly. And he can
shoot the eye out of a hawk. You know him.'

'Who is he?' said Tumulty slowly.

'The Gutty,' said McDara.

Tumulty started violently.

'Fetch!' he exclaimed. 'Do ye mean to say . . . ?'

'What?'

'One o' the worst thugs . . .'

'What of it?'

'Yer coddin'.'

'You don't think he's right?'

'Right? Why, the son of a . . .'

'Hold on now, Frank. He was good enough to save yer life in 1920 when he carried ye on his back out an ambush, two miles, and the blood coming in streams from a wound in yer thigh. What?'

Tumulty swelled out his chest and looked into the fire.

'That's true enough,' he mumbled, 'but . . .'

'But what?' snapped McDara.

'He went wrong once. He'll go wrong again. I know he got you out of camp. But . . . He's got a bad record. That fellah 'd drink whisky out of a sewer.'

'Damn his record,' whispered McDara furiously. 'What do I care about his record? I want a man that can fight. Fight. A tiger. Damn records. I don't give a damn if the fellow ripped his mother's heart out, provided . . .'

He clutched Tumulty's arm viciously and added:

'Provided he hates hard enough to go through blood and fire to get his enemy.'

Tumulty looked hard into McDara's blazing eyes. His underlip quivered.

'There's another reason for choosing Gutty,' said McDara with a subtle smile. 'I dug him up deliberately in New York for that reason.'

'What's that?' said Tumulty.

'I want to implicate everybody in this,' said

McDara, still smiling. 'Fetch was a tout for the fellow we're going to crease. There are a lot of these ex-thugs hanging around. Supposing anybody spots us . . . Well!'

'You mean they'll think that . . .'

'Aye,' said McDara, 'they'll think the whole country is united to crush the reptile.'

He laughed dryly, a sort of cackle.

'Tell me,' said Tumulty suddenly, with an awed look in his eyes.

'What?' said McDara.

'Do you believe in God?'

'Now what's he driving at?' thought McDara. 'This fellow is a proper mutt.'

'Why do you ask that question?' said McDara.

Tumulty frowned and said:

'No reason. Where is Fetch?'

'Not far from here.'

Tumulty squeezed his hands under his arms. Then he jumped to his feet. McDara also rose. He stood close beside Tumulty, looking up at him. It seemed as if he were prepared to seize Tumulty and prevent his escape. Tumulty began to mutter.

'What's that?' said McDara.

'I suppose he's all right,' said Tumulty.

'Listen,' said McDara with great force. 'Do you want to back out?'

'By the great God Almighty,' hissed Tumulty, raising his arm and making the sign of the Cross in the air, 'I've said yes and I mean yes.'

'Ha!' said McDara.

'Aye,' said Tumulty. He was trembling with passion. His eyes had become bloodshot. 'I've wasted my life fighting for the freedom of my fellow-man and I'm going to have my revenge. By . . .'

He caught up his chair violently in his hand. His mouth quivered. His chest was heaving. The man was writhing with passion. McDara seized his arm and whispered:

'Hey, hey! What the blazes are you doing? Keep quiet, can't you?'

'Eh?' said Tumulty, in a listless voice. 'All right. I'll get hold of the boys. When are we to meet? Mac! This job must get finished quick.'

'It's the same thing,' thought McDara. 'The two are the same.'

'This is Thursday,' he said aloud. 'Can you get your men together to-morrow and report to me to-morrow night? I might have the other information by then. Probably will. Then we can do the job on Sunday.'

'Get it, get it,' muttered Tumulty, 'and let's get done with it. I've been waiting long enough.'

'Right, then,' said McDara. 'At ten o'clock to-morrow night. Be at the foot of the Wellington Monument in the Phœnix Park. I'll meet ye there. Fetch 'll be there too. If I'm late, wait for me. That right?'

Tumulty bowed his head and said:

'All right.'

123

'Well!' said McDara. 'Shake hands on it, Frank.'

They clasped hands, looking into one another's eyes.

'Frank,' said McDara, 'do you remember that night we were sitting up in the tree, with the English soldiers prowling around down below looking for us? And we whispering up there, like two crows. I remember that night you said that the great dream of your life was to do some single act that would set the whole country ablaze. Well . . . here it is.'

Tumulty's eyes grew dreamy. McDara whispered dreamily:

'And the two of us are together again, Frank.'

Tumulty caught McDara by both arms and they looked longingly into one another's eyes. Then, without another word, McDara left the room. Tumulty remained behind.

Half-way down the stairs McDara halted and said to himself:

'This is very strange. Do I really believe it? How long will it last? What will it be like afterwards? Neither of them believed it. Each has his own God. Have I none, then? Christ! It's going to be terrible afterwards.'

With his head fallen on his breast, he continued to go down slowly. The powerful voice was still shouting in the room below. It was saying: 'Now, look here, Mary. Either I have my beer or I'll knock the two eyes out o' yer head. Where would I hide the money? I tell ye I had only a bob on each way.'

He left the house and went towards the shop where Fetch lived. Fetch was waiting for him in the shop. They went outside and stood at the corner. Fetch appeared to be half drunk.

'Been drinking?' said McDara.

'All right,' said Fetch in a cross voice. 'Ye needn't worry about that. My mouth is a tomb, drunk or sober. I got windy about the spooks. A few drinks set me right again.'

'All right. To-morrow night, ten o'clock, Wellington Monument in the park.'

'Yes. I got ye. Say, though. Did you see Frank?'

McDara nodded.

'Tell him about me?'

McDara nodded.

'What did he say?' asked Fetch.

'He said: "Remember the night Gutty carried me on his back, an' I wounded in the thigh?" '

'Poor ole Frank,' said Fetch.

He struck his gloved hands together and tapped the pavement with his toe.

'Poor ole Frank,' he repeated. 'I was a son of a gun, Mac, to quit that old crowd. But . . . we'll get our own back. When do you think it'll come off?'

'Sunday, I think,' said McDara. 'Listen. Got any money left?'

Fetch shook his head. McDara handed him a five-pound note.

'That'll see ye right till to-morrow night. We divvy up then.'

Fetch clutched the note and then took McDara's hand. He spoke with a broken voice:

'Mac, old son,' he began.

But McDara cut him short gruffly.

'That'll do, Gutty,' he said. 'Forget it. Ten o'clock to-morrow night. Don't forget.'

They parted.

McDara walked away very rapidly, swinging his arms and walking without a stoop in his shoulders.

'Curse these fellows,' he kept saying. 'Curse everybody. Why can't I find a man that sees and feels like I do, somebody with a heart like a stone? Christ! I want to leap from a high mountain into the midst of space. If we only believed it, we could toss the earth about like a toy. Curse it! Curse it! The earth is peopled with crawling worms.'

Suddenly he shivered, looked about him with fear and bent his head forward. He put his hands in his pockets, slackened his steps and carefully stooped his shoulders.

CHAPTER TEN

It was after eleven o'clock when McDara reached his room. He went to bed at once and fell asleep. He slept like a log. He did not awaken until nine o'clock the following morning. When he awoke he felt exhausted. He lay on his back, staring at the ceiling of the room, unable even to think.

His body seemed to be numb. When he moved his feet or his hands, ever so slightly, he was forced to make a noise with his lips, as if with the pain of moving a fractured limb. That lasted for half an hour. Then the numbness left him and a corresponding agility took possession of his body. He wanted to jump up at once and dance around the room. He restrained this desire, got out of bed and dressed slowly.

He washed, shaved and combed his hair very carefully. He kept smiling all the while. When he had finished dressing, he thought of having breakfast. But he did not feel at all hungry. He smiled also at the thought of having food.

'But I must,' he said to himself. 'I must eat.'

He stood in the middle of the floor and folded his arms.

'I'll have an enormous meal,' he said to himself. 'I'll rest all day to-day. There's nothing to do. I'll keep away from Fetch. There is no sense in bothering him to-day. He'll drink all day. It's only in that state, after heavy drinking, that he can get into the mood. Then he'll be a devil. If I go near him he might turn on me. Tumulty is all right too. He likes being a conspirator. He'll simply love running around after his ten men. From to-morrow night, though, when it's coming near the time . . . that'll be the time to watch him. I'll mount guard over him with Fetch.'

He rubbed his chin. An extraordinary gaiety was compelling him to keep smiling. He lit the gas-fire and put on the kettle. He put eggs, bacon and sausages in a pan, ready to cook. Then he began to walk around the room again.

Something kept throbbing in his mind. Then he could feel a little red ball, circling round and round inside his skull. That did not hurt, because it was smiling as it circled round and round. He also circled round and round the floor, keeping time with its movement. He touched things, here and there, as he walked round and round, the bedpost, the face of a girl on the wallpaper, the window curtain, the mantelpiece.

The kettle boiled. He licked his palm with his tongue, rolled up his sleeves and cooked his breakfast. He sat down to table and ate an enormous meal. Then he felt sated.

'I won't go out at all,' he said. 'I'll think here all day. That will be nice. Let me see. What's it like outside?'

He looked out the window. It was dry, but very gloomy. A little down the street, on the far side, workmen were placing scaffolding against the wall of a house. He began to watch them work.

The servant came in to clean the room. When she saw him leaning against the window, she started and said:

'Sorry, Mr. Carter, I thought ye were gone out.'

'Go ahead,' he said.

He watched her stupid face, as she began to fumble about the room. He saw her look at the remains of the bacon and sausages on his plate.

'Oh! Good Lord!' he said. 'I never thought of this being Friday. It is Friday, isn't it?'

'Yes,' she said. 'It's Friday. Are you a Catholic, Mr. Carter?'

'Of course,' he said. 'What did ye think I'd be?'

She looked at him in a friendly way.

'That's awful,' he said. 'I think there's nothing more awful than breaking the fast. I'm sure Mrs. Buggy 'll think I'm a regular pagan.'

'Oh! Indeed she won't, Mr. Carter,' said the maid. 'Sure it was only a mistake. An' I thought maybe ye were a Protestant.'

'No fear. Ye'll see me trotting off to confession to-morrow night,' he said, 'and to Communion on Sunday morning. The pro-Cathedral is the nearest Church to here, isn't it?'

'No. Gardiner Street is nearer,' she said. 'Did ye hear of a job yet?'

'I have a good chance of one,' he answered.

'There's an old colonel here that I knew in France and he promised to get me one.'

'I'm glad to hear that, Mr. Carter,' she said.

She left the room. He winked.

'That's a good dodge,' he said to himself, when she had gone. 'Every little thing counts. I mustn't forget that telegram, though. That's very important.'

The thought of the telegram made him feel serious. The servant had set the fire. He lit it, put a newspaper in front of it and sat down by the hearth.

'Afterwards,' he thought. 'What about that?'

His face grew dark. A great cavern opened up before his mind and he gazed into the cavern with horror. There was nothing there. His muscles became rigid. His face scowled. He felt himself rising up, with his right hand stretched out, saying:

'Why have I been created out of nothing and know nothing? Who has wrought my bones and flesh from nothing and given me a mind to look upon this infinity that it cannot understand?'

A little wheel began to revolve in his skull, instead of the red spot that had circled round in it a little while ago. This wheel caused him pain, like an unpleasant drug. He sank into a stupor, during which he became painfully conscious of the movements of the little wheel, each cog of which grated painfully against the walls of his skull. His mind was fixed on a naked man, rising out of loam and holding his hands aloft to the sky. Something was dragging him down. He was sinking gradually, but very slowly,

130

into a seething pool of silver mire. His face was in agony, but there was an exalted look in his eyes. He was looking at something of infinite beauty, which was just beyond the reach of his upraised hands.

McDara contemplated this struggling man for a long time. His nostrils kept twitching. Then he stretched out his hand, grasped suddenly at the empty air with his fingers and started. The vision vanished. He threw back his head and smiled. His mind came back to reality.

'I am breaking under the strain,' he thought. 'What shall I do? Shall I go out and drink? What about the landlady, though? What time is it?'

He took a large silver watch from his waistcoat-pocket and looked at it. Heavens! It was nearly one o'clock. How long had he been looking at that vision? Hours!

He threw himself on the bed and fell asleep at once. He awoke at four o'clock feeling refreshed and happy. He lay on the bed for a little while after awaking. Then he got to the floor and thought:

'I must finish with the landlady now. It's best settle that point now. Everything else is in order. I wonder is she gone out?'

He went to the door, opened it and looked out over the banisters. He heard the landlady down-stairs talking to another lodger, who was going out. He went back into his room, leaving the door slightly ajar. He waited for some time, wondering what was the best means of approaching her. Fortune supplied the means. The landlady herself came upstairs. He closed the door and waited inside until he heard her steps on the landing outside. Then he suddenly opened the door and came out on to the landing. He collided with her. He put his hand on her arm and begged her pardon.

'I'm awfully sorry, Mrs. Buggy,' he said. 'I was just . . .'

Then he smiled on her as he had done in the kitchen and without letting go her arm. He flushed and pretended to become embarrassed. Then he looked at his hand, took it away and flushed still more. The landlady smiled back at him.

'You didn't go out to-day,' she said in a low voice.

'No,' he said. 'I'm terribly excited. I'm expecting a job. Colonel Johnson, whom I met in France, has promised to get me a job, but . . .'

He paused and lowered his eyes.

'We can't have everything our own way. I might have to leave Dublin.'

The landlady's face grew suspicious and angry. She looked at him coldly. He suddenly caught her hand and pressed it.

'Maybe 'twould be better after all,' he said, with his face close to hers, 'than staying here . . . in the same house with you. I'm afraid of you. I'm terribly lonely and . . .'

He began to press her hand excitedly, looking fiercely into her eyes. He made a movement towards her, as if to seize her in his arms. Then he muttered something violently and dashed into his room. He listened inside the door. She did not move. He opened the door again. She was still there, with a smile on her face.

'For God's sake, Mrs. Buggy,' he said, 'forgive me.'

She laughed and came quite close to him.

'What are ye afraid of?' she said in a low voice.

He became aware of her taut breasts and of her powerful body, which had suddenly become imbued with a great sensual charm. His pretended embarrassment became real. He wanted to seize her in his arms and carry her into his room. But he remained still, flushing.

She poked his side with her bare elbow and said, with a giggle:

'Well! I'll be blowed. A young fellah like you. I'll be blowed.'

Still he remained silent. Then suddenly he threw his arms around her and clasped her tightly. She did not struggle. He did not kiss her, however. As soon as his arms closed about her heavy body, a feeling of repulsion overcame him. He looked beyond her shoulder at the wall, stuck out his tongue and grinned. He loosed her and fled into his room. She followed him in, still smiling.

He sat down on his bed, looking at her gloomily.

'What about your friend that came to see ye the other night?' she said.

He started.

133

'Oh! Miss Todd,' he said. 'She's connected with the Legion. I was her brother's batman in France. He was killed. It's she is trying to get me the job. In fact, I expect her this evening with definite news.'

The landlady remained silent, standing with her arms folded, as if expecting something further. But he made no movement. Then the landlady laughed and waved her arms.

'You fellows are all the same,' she said. 'The war knocked all the . . . Well! What d'ye think o' that now? Who'd ever believe it? An old woman.'

She paused again and looked at him, smiling broadly. He looked back at her.

'If I did it,' he thought, 'she'd be mad when I went away and probably talk. But if I keep quiet now, she'll be fascinated.'

He did not move. Then she approached him slowly, ruffled his hair with her hand and said:

'Don't be put out, sonny. Yer only a boy. D'ye hear?'

He buried his face in his hands. Then she sighed and walked to the door.

'Ah! Well!' she said. 'It's a sad world.'

She went out and closed the door softly behind her. Then he jumped to his feet.

'Good!' he exclaimed. 'That's settled too. But why this terrible preparation for the aftermath? Suicide would be better. There'll be nothing but one long . . . Or what will it really be like?'

He prepared another meal and devoured it ravenously.

At ten minutes past seven o'clock the landlady again came to the door and said the lady wanted to see him.

'Tell her to come up,' he said.

CHAPTER ELEVEN

KITTY MELLETT came into the room, dressed exactly as she had been dressed on her previous visit. As soon as she had closed the door, McDara came up to her, took her by both hands and drew her up to the fire.

'Well!' he said excitedly.

'Leave me alone a moment,' she said quietly.

He stepped back and looked at her. She seemed perfectly unconcerned. She slowly took off her glasses and put them in her coat pocket. She took off her coat, her cap and then her gloves, which she folded, one within the other, and put them on the mantelpiece. Then she calmly went to the mirror and tidied her hair.

He watched her, a trifle uneasily. At last she came up to him and held out her hands.

'I've done my work,' she said in a low voice, dramatically. 'Now, it's up to you to lead. But I must be in it too. I want to tell you that now. I want to run the same risk as you. Otherwise it would be immoral for me to take part in it.'

'What are you talking about?' he said. 'Did you find out whether he'll be guarded or not?'

She sat down by the fire and held her hands to the flames. He sat down beside her, still looking at her curiously. She looked very beautiful, but there were dark rings under her grey eyes.

'She's getting windy, too,' he thought. 'That's why she wants to take part in it.'

'No,' she said quietly. 'He'll be unguarded. It will be just like slaughtering a bull.'

She spoke dreamily, coldly, as if she were half drunk, or else on the verge of hysterics. All her body, except her throat, was perfectly motionless, almost limp. Her throat twitched. He watched, wrinkling his nose.

'Come, tell me,' he said nervously. 'Are you sure? Tell me.'

She looked at him sideways.

'So you'd funk it,' she said, 'if he had a guard. I wouldn't, though.'

'Is she gone mad?' he thought.

'No,' she repeated. 'He'll be unguarded. Why did I go to all this trouble to find out he's unguarded for the slaughter? It's immoral to slaughter a man like a bull. However, I must go through with it now. I'll do it myself.'

'God!' he thought. 'What a situation! She's gone out of her mind.'

'Come on,' he said aloud. 'Tell me about it. Who told you? Are you certain he's unguarded? Is your information reliable? Can't you see it's very important for us to know?'

She looked at him sideways again.

'Who's us?' she said.

He caught her limp hand. It was ice-cold.

'Do you feel ill?' he said.

She did not reply. She stared him in the face with vacant eyes. She shuddered and looked into the fire.

Then an idea flashed into his mind. He lowered his head and opened his lips. His eyes gleamed. With a quick movement he threw his arms about her, held her tightly and whispered:

'Kitty, Kitty, why do you torture me like this? I . . . I . . . I'm exhausted.'

He held his face close to the back of her neck and listened. He felt her body quiver. Then it became warm. For some moments she made no movement. Then he heard her say: 'Oh! God!' Then she began to struggle to free herself. He released her, drew back and went on one knee in front of her. He took her right hand in both of his and began to caress it.

'What's been troubling you, Kitty?' he said.

'What's that?' she said angrily.

With an angry expression on her face, she looked up and down his face, from his forehead to his lips and back again. Then she wiped her left eye with the back of her free hand.

'Let go my hand,' she said.

He went to his chair and sat down.

'I'll leave her alone for a minute,' he thought.

They sat in silence. She kept looking into the fire, quivering spasmodically. He watched her, trying to catch an expression in her face that would allow him to attack her again.

At last she began to describe the meeting with Carmody in the Shelbourne Hotel. She began in a low voice and related what happened until she left the hotel with him. Then suddenly she burst into tears and mumbled through her tears:

'He excited me so much, I wanted to die . . . to kill him . . . to kill him. Oh! God! Aren't you a monster to sit there in cold blood and make me go through all that? I must do it now, myself, to have revenge for what . . .'

She stopped suddenly, caught McDara by the arm and said sharply:

'He didn't do what you think. Do you hear?'

McDara lost patience with her and said through his teeth:

'I don't give a single damn what he DID. I want to know what he *said*.'

'Oh!' she said.

She began to shiver and shrugged her shoulders several times.

'I'm giving you my word of honour that he'll have no guard,' she said in a queer tone. 'Isn't that enough for you?'

He scowled.

'What's at the back of her mind?' he thought. 'Do I know that fellow Carmody? Supposing he bought her over?'

'That's good enough for me,' he said aloud.

'Very well, then,' she said, rubbing her palms together. 'Proceed.'

'Proceed about what?'

'When is it going to be done? I'm at your service.

139

Your cunning has helped you to make all these plans. Finish them. Do you see this bag?'

She held up a little embroidered handbag. It was shaped almost like an oyster-shell.

'I've carried bombs in that,' she said. 'I can carry a gun in it too. I suppose we'll slaughter him with a gun.'

'In the name of . . .' he began.

'What?' she interrupted, looking at him wildly. 'Surely you don't think you're going to do it?'

'Yes. I'm going to do it,' she replied.

He lay back in his chair. The chair creaked.

'What am I to do with her?' he thought.

'All right,' he said suddenly. 'Do it. I wash my hands of it. I leave here to-morrow morning. You have betrayed me to your friend Carmody.'

She looked up at him in amazement. He pretended to be very excited; but it was impossible to discern from his cold, glittering eyes what was passing in his mind. She looked into his eyes, trying to probe down into his soul. And as she failed to pierce beneath their icy blue surface, her lips began a trembling movement. Slowly she leaned forward towards him, held out her hands and then sank hurriedly to her knees. She clutched his body and clawed at the buttons of his coat.

'Don't leave me, Michael,' she said, looking up at him, with her mouth open.

He remained silent. She looked away from him and then looked back suddenly. She smiled. Then

140

her attitude changed completely. She became quite calm and self-possessed. She spoke in a gentle voice, coyly.

'It's because I know you'll go away afterwards,' she said. 'Then I'll be alone again. It's going to be the same as before. The people are not going to rise. You should have seen them at the Shelbourne, Carmody and McShiel and Tynum. They have no souls. They are as cold as ice. They just laugh at us. They'll exploit anything that happens. Carmody is just like . . . the man that's going to be slaughtered. He, or somebody else like him, will step into the dead man's shoes. The next day perhaps or later.'

McDara made a movement with his teeth as if he were chewing. His eyes blinked. He looked sideways, raised his eyebrows and scowled.

'Don't you see?' she said, trembling. She stroked his knee with her fingers.

'No,' he said. 'I don't see.'

'What?' she said, opening her eyes wide.

McDara got to his feet and stretched down his hands by his sides, breathing heavily through his nose.

'I don't want the people to rise,' he said. 'I'm not a Communist. What do I care about the people?'

Then he uttered a savage exclamation and folded his arms.

'The greatest folly that has grown in the human mind is this Christian worship of the slave, this bastard humanitarianism. It's a lie, a silly, sentimental lie, seeing peasants marching with blood on their banners. I didn't see it.'

Kitty looked at him in amazement. He glanced at her, raised his eyebrows, as if in pain, and then laughed. He sat down again. He held out his right palm and began to strike it with his left forefinger.

'Listen, Kitty,' he said. 'I didn't really tell you why I am going to do this. I didn't tell anybody, not even myself.'

They looked at one another.

'I know it now, though,' he added.

Her eyes became strained. Her lips blubbered and she held out her hands to him.

'Take me away with you, Michael,' she said in a broken whisper.

He apparently did not hear her, because he said:

'I am doing this because I want to be free. To cut every cord. It's only when a man cuts every cord that he approaches nearest to being a God. Supposing, then, a man arises, who is so far beyond the comprehension of his mates, in fearlessness, in bru –'

He stopped suddenly and looked down at her cunningly.

'What did you say?' he said excitedly.

'Where are you going?' she said.

'How do you mean?'

'Afterwards.'

He paused.

'You don't want to do it now. You've changed your mind.'

'No,' she said wearily. 'I'm tired. I'm tired looking at my mother. She accuses me.'

'Then you'll stay quiet and say nothing. Very quiet.'

'Oh! Christ! Tell me, tell me, Michael, where are you going afterwards? Are you going to take me? You can tear yourself free. I can't. I no longer believe anything.'

'Supposing . . .' he began.

Then he paused and looked at her fiercely.

'What?' she said.

'Supposing, after all,' he continued slowly, 'that he changes his mind and has a guard and . . . I get killed. Then, how do you mean, where would I go?'

They looked at one another tensely.

'Is that what you mean?' he whispered.

She sat back on her heels, on the floor. Her head sank on her chest.

'No, no,' she muttered, 'I don't mean anything. Nothing at all.'

He went on his knees beside her and took her in his arms. Without moving, or trying to disengage herself, she kept muttering:

'Don't touch me. Let me alone.'

Tears came into his eyes and the two personalities again came to life in him. One shed tears and longed to kiss her and to kneel beside her, praying, howling out to God. The other scowled and thought:

'Use force. Be violent. She's hysterical. She'll keep quiet, though.'

Then another idea occurred to him. And he whispered:

'You're tired, Kitty. Go home and rest. Listen. I'll take you away. Listen. You won't have to stay here afterwards. Listen. Are you listening?'

She slowly raised her head.

CHAPTER TWELVE

McDara was the first to arrive at the Wellington Monument. It was very dark. There were no stars. The moon had not yet risen. The night was dry and chilly. The grass was crisp. Footsteps made a swishing sound over it. On the roadways, all round, in the vast park, footsteps crunched, crunched, going in all directions. Lovers marched, arm in arm, seeking a quiet place for their amorous embraces. There were occasional peals of laughter, cat-calls, whistles and then . . . the continual crunch, crunch of feet, marching hurriedly.

In the darkness, the sounds of footsteps, innumerable sounds of footsteps, caused McDara to become very excited, as he waited for his confederates at the base of the Monument.

The shadows of tall trees swept away into the horizon. The park looked like a forest in the darkness. There was the same strange silence there, as in a forest, with the pat-pat of feet, of wild beasts' feet, moving continually. The city had become remote. The huge Monument rose above him, mysterious in the darkness, like a pyramid in the desert of Egypt.

Then he distinguished Tumulty's footsteps among the sounds that reached his ears from the distance. Tumulty always struck the ground sharply with his heels, with regular beats like a soldier of a Guards regiment. One could count the time, second by second, with his footbeats. He struck the earth with great power, as if hammering nails into the ground.

The sound of Tumulty's steps made McDara start with pride and he saw again, on the banks of the Po, Hasdrubal's Nubian horsemen, caparisoned, with thundering hoofs. His lungs expanded and he threw back his head. He thought with pride that historians would use great rhetoric to describe this deed. Suddenly he wanted, instead of flight, to carry the blood-stained head through the city and show it to the people. 'This is the head of the tyrant.'

Tumulty's footsteps left the path and swished over the crisp grass. They halted at the Monument near McDara. His figure stood out, black and square in the darkness. McDara approached him. McDara's figure was like that of a ghost, a body wide at the base, tapering upwards, stooping forward at the shoulders, with a forward-reaching head. When the figures were side by side, McDara coughed and said:

'Excuse me, have ye got a match?'

'That Mac?'

They shook hands. McDara noted that Tumulty's fingers squeezed nervously with great force. His voice was dry and strained.

'Gutty come yet?'

'No. Not yet.'

They went to the steps of the Monument and sat down. McDara became still more excited with the romance of the forthcoming act. The presence of Tumulty's body beside him in the darkness height-

146

ened his consciousness of the similarity between his
intended act and other great deeds that had stood
out in history. Why? Strength. Tumulty's breath
came through his nostrils in strong gusts. A choker
of throats. Laocoön. A man entwined with snakes.
The naked man springing from the loam of silver
mire.

McDara, sitting in the darkness beside Tumulty,
saw man, with a shining body, stalking the firmament, with the conquered earth on his back, seeking
other spheres to loot.

'Hey!' said Tumulty in an angry whisper.

His heavy breathing stopped. McDara drew back
his head and listened.

'What?'

'Who the hell put out that yarn?' said Tumulty
savagely.

'What yarn?'

'I met that crazy fellah Dignum in Fleet Street,
coming out of the Palace. He shouted out: "There's
Tumulty. What did ye do to the girl from Westmeath?" It's all round town that I seduced a girl
from Westmeath and that she's after me and that
that's why I was fired out of the volunteers.'

McDara paused and then he smiled.

'Good!' he said. 'I thought it might be something
else.'

'How d'ye mean?'

'I was wondering what made yer fingers quiver.
That's all to the good.'

'What? D'ye think I'm goin' to let these . . .'

'Have sense, man. It might save yer life. That's a useful rumour. A man that's chasing women has no thought for . . . more important things. I hope they notify the police.'

'That be damned!' said Tumulty savagely. 'If I catch the son of a gun that put out the rumour . . . I'll . . .'

'What'll you do to him?' said McDara.

'I'll wring his neck.'

'Go ahead,' said McDara. 'Here is the man beside you.'

Tumulty became silent.

'I told Kitty Mellett to spread that rumour,' continued McDara. 'I didn't want people to be wondering why she was looking for you. Now, that's all to the good. In face of the bigger thing, they'll forget your affair afterwards. In the meantime, you'll escape suspicion. Ye see. . . . After this act, the Republicans might line up with the Government, in order to save their necks, and if they do . . . well, it would go hard with expelled members.'

Tumulty remained silent. Then he muttered at length:

'God! Mac, you're a . . . you're a . . . you're a . . . you've a gift either from God or the devil.'

McDara laughed and said:

'Let's say the devil. Here he comes.'

Fetch was approaching. His footsteps hardly made any sound on the grass. His figure was twisted about, giving the impression, in the darkness, that he was going in several directions, or zigzagging from side to side in a drunken manner.

He walked up boldly to the two men at the base of the Monument. He sat down beside them. He brought a smell of alcohol with him.

'Well, fellahs!' he said in a cheery voice. 'What's the verdict? Is the coffin ordered?'

He had sat down beside McDara. He leaned across McDara and held out his hand to Tumulty.

'Shake, Frank,' he said, in a laughing voice. 'It's a long time since we've met.'

McDara dug his elbow into Tumulty's ribs. Tumulty took the hand and clasped it.

'That's the ticket,' said Fetch.

Then he put his elbows on his knees and rapped his gloved hands together. McDara began to talk immediately.

'We all know what we're here for,' he said. 'So we might as well begin.'

'That's the ticket,' said Fetch. 'No need to discuss the weather.'

'Half a mo',' said Tumulty gruffly. 'Don't rush things. This is a serious business. I'm not casting any aspersions on anybody, but I'd like things done properly. There was a time when we were all comrades on the same flying column. We were sworn in then. We better be sworn in now too.'

'Yer not hintin' at anything, Frank?' said Fetch angrily.

'For God's sake,' said McDara, 'chuck that!'

He spoke with great force. He felt the bodies, on either side of him, quiver.

'Swear if you like. Go ahead, but don't start trying to hide anything that's in your mind, Frank, with roundabout innuendoes.'

Tumulty remained silent.

'Well!' continued McDara. 'Begin the swearing. I'm ready.'

Fetch uttered an oath and said:

'So am I. So help me God.'

'I want things done properly,' grumbled Tumulty.

'I know what's in his mind, Mac,' said Fetch. 'He thinks I'm . . .'

'You keep quiet, Gutty,' said McDara. 'Nobody thinks anything. If you two fellows are funky about it . . .'

'I never funked anything in my life,' said Tumulty. 'I'm not going to do it now either.'

'Well! What's all the talk about, then?' said McDara. 'Do you think I'm going to funk it?'

'No,' said Tumulty.

'Who, then?' said McDara.

With a sudden movement, Fetch pulled an automatic pistol out of his breast, held it out towards Tumulty and said:

'You an' I swore on that once. Go ahead.'

McDara grasped Fetch's arm and said fiercely:

'Put away that gun, you fool. Put it away, blast it!'

Fetch put back the pistol into his breast.

'Listen, men,' said Tumulty. 'I . . . Well! I don't like this job being rushed like this. That's all. This wants long considering.'

'And you listen to me,' said McDara fiercely. 'You're in this now, Tumulty, and, by God, you stay in it! See? Nobody tricks with me. I've considered this job for three years. I've sweated to save enough money to carry it through. I've racked my brains to make a plan. I've made it watertight. I've put the proposition to you. You've agreed. So has Gutty. And you two are going to go through with it, or by . . .'

He trembled and then became rigid.

'Mac, Mac,' whispered Tumulty.

'Go ahead, son,' said Fetch. 'That's talk.'

Tumulty leaned across McDara towards Fetch and growled:

'Don't you get cocky, Gutty. I've done . . .'

'*Keep quiet*,' hissed McDara. 'You're in it now. So put a sock in it.'

The three men became silent.

'Here,' said McDara, unbuttoning his raincoat.

'Watch now,' he thought; 'this should do the work.'

Both men watched his hands eagerly, as he unbuttoned his raincoat. He did it slowly. Then he took out his note-case. Both men started slightly when they saw the note-case. He took off the rubber band. He opened the case and took out a bundle of five-pound notes that were folded at the middle. He closed the case, put on the rubber band and put the case back into his pocket. Holding the notes in one hand, he slowly buttoned up his raincoat with the other.

'Now,' he said, 'we'll begin operations. There should be twenty of these notes here.'

He slowly began to count. When he reached ten, he divided the bundle. He counted the other half. There were ten there also. He put a little bundle in each hand, held one towards Tumulty and the other towards Fetch.

'There's fifty for each of you,' he said. 'Put that in your pockets.'

Fetch grabbed at the notes, flicked them against his thumb and clicked his tongue. He stuffed them into his coat pocket and kept his hand in the pocket with them. Tumulty hesitated, looking at the notes.

'Go on, Frank,' said McDara, 'I'll explain.'

Tumulty stretched out his hand and took the notes. McDara brushed his two palms together.

'That is in case anything happens before the job is done,' he said. 'After the job is done, if everything is all right, each will receive fifty more. Everybody satisfied?'

'O.K. far as I'm concerned,' said Fetch eagerly.

'And you, Frank?'

Tumulty was toying with the notes.

'Yes,' he lisped, almost inaudibly.

'Well, now,' said McDara. 'Let's go ahead. I got the other information. He'll have no guard.'

'Is that right?' said Tumulty eagerly.

'Hush,' said McDara, 'don't speak so loud.'

'Guard be damned!' said Fetch. 'I'd crease twenty of them before they'd know what hit them.'

'There's no guard,' continued McDara, 'unless something unforeseen happens.' He turned to Tumulty. 'Like one of your men making some blunder.'

'No fear o' that,' said Tumulty eagerly.

Tumulty's manner had entirely changed. He was now very enthusiastic. He leaned forward and put his elbows on his knees. His powerful jaws stood out in the darkness.

'We have taped six cars,' he drawled, in a nasal tone, slowly. 'We can lift them any time, either to-night or to-morrow night, and we have stalls for them too.'

'Right,' said McDara. 'Three, I said, not six.'

'We'll take three,' said Tumulty, in a low whisper, through his nose, rubbing his palms together.

'Listen,' said Fetch. 'Make it a Ford. Say, I'll have to have a deck at all three and pick out the best. I'll have to be on this job. We don't want a crock.'

'Leave that to me. These are no crocks. You can have a Ford if ye like.'

'Yes, a Ford,' said Fetch. 'I saw a new Ford drawn up exactly on the spot where I'll be parked.

Savvy? Some fellah on that road uses a Ford. They'll think it's the same Ford.'

'That's all right,' said McDara. 'Now about weapons.'

'I'm fixed,' said Fetch. 'I got my daisy here.'

He tapped his breast.

'I told you not to carry that around with you,' said McDara.

'Nothing stirring,' said Fetch. 'Ye don't catch me knockin' around without a weapon.'

He coughed and added:

'Nobody is goin' to get me alive . . . not if I know anything.'

'I've got mine,' said Tumulty, still rubbing his palms together and speaking almost inaudibly. 'I think a long-nosed Smith an' Wesson 'd be best for a job like this.'

'What can you get for me?' said McDara. 'I've got nothing.'

'I've got a good Webley,' said Tumulty.

'That'll do,' said McDara. 'Have it ready to-morrow evening.'

'Very well, then,' he continued, after a pause. 'Let's go ahead.'

'What about that girl?' said Tumulty. 'Kitty Mellett.'

'How d'ye mean?'

'Have you . . . No fear of her letting anything . . .'

'Now, for God sake,' said McDara, 'don't start

154

again. What d'ye want? Jam on it? We have to take chances. This is not a picnic. She's all right. I just left her. I fixed her all right.'

'Don't get ratty,' said Tumulty. 'I know her of old. She might just crop up on the scene, at the very moment, and spoil everything.'

'She won't,' said McDara. 'She doesn't know when it's going to be done.'

'That's the next point,' said Tumulty. 'When is it?'

'Eleven o'clock,' said McDara. 'Are you dead sure, Gutty, that you've got the spot all right?'

'I can give ye the exact measurement,' said Fetch. 'Including the number of rails opposite the little orchard and the number of blocks in the pavements.'

'All right, then. Well. You drive, Fetch. Frank an' I'll . . . We'll look after the other part.'

Fetch beat his gloved palms together and said viciously:

'We'll all have a shot at that part of the work.'

'Now, look here,' said McDara. 'No breaking of any part of the programme, Gutty.'

'Listen, Mac,' said Fetch. 'Everything above board. I'm ready to drive the bus, but . . . but . . . I've waited some time to get this bird. I'm goin' to have revenge. I'm goin' to dance in that fellow's guts. Don't anybody try to stop me. Anyway, you couldn't hit a haystack at ten yards.'

McDara was going to reply when Tumulty said gloomily:

'That part of the business 'll be all right, but what I want to know is this . . . will the people rise?'

'Eh?' said McDara. 'What people?'

'The people,' said Tumulty. 'The common people. If I thought that this job would have no effect like that, I . . .'

'What effect?' snapped McDara.

'Ah! God Almighty!' said Tumulty, with an accent of despair in his voice. 'Why trick with words like this? It's easy to play that game, pretending to be heartless. But you as well as me feel the lack of something here' – he put his hand on his heart and clutched at his coat. 'Years ago we had something here and now it's not here.'

He stopped. McDara stared in front of him. Again he heard the blare of trumpets on the Po. The romance of war rose up before his mind, the joy of conquest, the fanatical enthusiasm of people marching, singing the 'Marseillaise.'

Then he heard Fetch snuffling. And Fetch said: 'What you said right now, Frank, reminds me. . . . It's a son of a gun, but . . . Christ! A man 'd be better off roasting in hell than living like this without . . .'

He tried to finish his sentence, failed and then struck his gloved hands together violently. The three men became silent. A curious emotion took possession of them. McDara joined in this emotion, although his mind kept warning him to keep it at a distance and not to succumb to it.

Some invisible and indescribable force drew them close together and then fired them with a melancholy ardour for an ideal, which they could not express.

In the darkness, their three sombre figures, huddled at the base of the Monument, sitting in silence, became ghoulish. But their souls soared up into a fantastic realm, pursuing a phantom, which they tried in vain to catch, disrobe and ravish. That was Heaven, the goal of human dreams, where all things are good and beautiful.

Then Tumulty said:

'I'd like to die like that, leading the people. I think it would be a great thing to fall down, with blood pouring from yer wounds, and feel the feet of the people trampling on yer dying body and they rushing forward, shouting.'

There was another heavy silence.

'Maybe they will too,' he said in a wild whisper. 'Maybe they'll rise too.'

McDara shuddered. Then he smiled secretly, looking away into the darkness. He saw a place of abandoned revelry, a drear place. He furrowed his forehead, contemplating it. The naked man, uttering a horrible moan, was swallowed up in a pool of silver mire. Then the empty darkness soothed his eyes and he smiled again.

Fetch began to snuffle.

'Listen, Frank,' he said, leaning across McDara. 'Ye've got no grudge against me, have ye? I declare to Almighty God, I was led astray. I knew no better.

I want to . . . I want to put myself right and . . .
It's a son of a gun.'

'Cut that out, Gutty,' said Tumulty.

'I say,' said McDara in a gloomy tone. 'We had
better finish this business. There's another matter
we have to settle before we meet to-morrow night.
That's clothes. You get hold of a new suit to-
morrow, Frank. Let me see. You should wear plus-
fours and a mackintosh with a belt. Can you get
them without arousing any suspicion? I mean . . .
get hold of them quietly . . . in some quiet shop.'

'Very well,' said Tumulty.

'You've got your suit, Gutty?'

'Yes,' said Fetch.

'Very well, then.'

They became silent once more.

'To-morrow evening at nine,' said McDara,
'we'll all meet in your room, Frank. That all right?'

That was agreed. Then they sat together in
silence once more. Suddenly McDara stretched out
his hands and grasped their knees.

'Comrades,' he said, in a throbbing voice, 'from
now on, it will be too late to think clearly. We'll be
intent on the job. This is maybe the last moment
we'll be together as man to man. And . . . I too feel
that same thing . . . what you were trying to say just
now. Well! I swear by my mother's grave that . . .'

He suddenly loosed their knees and jumped to
his feet. He stood, with drooping head. They rose
too and stood beside him, watching him.

'There's no use getting sentimental' he muttered. 'Better get out of here. Frank, you go first. Look after yourself until nine o'clock to-morrow night. So long, Frank.'

'So long, Mac,' said Tumulty, gripping his hand.

'I'll go along with Frank,' said Fetch, 'an' arrange about those cars.'

'Good night, Gutty,' said McDara.

They moved away over the grass. McDara sat down again at the base of the Monument with his chin in his hands, staring into the darkness.

CHAPTER THIRTEEN

THE wind began to whistle mournfully. He sat listening to it, as it came through the bare tree-trunks, over the midland plain, sweeping down towards the city, carrying a message of . . . death.

'Death!'

He rose to his feet and then moved away slowly, listening to the wind and allowing his mind to be carried with it, also mournful, whistling fantastic thoughts.

He walked all the way to his lodgings. And during that walk, he reached a state of great happiness. Life had become simple, eternal, attuned to a single, unchanging theme, a melancholy acceptance of the futility of endeavour. He walked as if he were a ghost, walled in by his non-existence from receiving any impression by contact with the sights, sounds and smells of the life about him. There was only one faculty of his mind active, the faculty that received the impression of the whistling wind, with its mournful cadence, the atmosphere of ghostliness, of non-existence.

And he looked like a monk as he walked, brooding over this thought of non-existence and futility, where all things merge into the contemplation of a white-robed God, sitting in idle splendour, with complacent countenance, surrounded with many self-begotten beings, also sitting in idle contemplation.

It was at that hour when all steps turn homewards

and when sounds are dulled by the approach of sleep and forgetfulness. In the windy streets, the dust and refuse were caught by the whirling gusts and carried along, in a gesture of contempt for the toil that man had expended that day, making castles in the sands. The black city, blackened by a lightless night, assumed a romantic beauty in his black mind. Shabby, emaciated, with feverish eyes and stooping shoulders, he walked with long, slack strides, through the empty streets, triumphant in his melancholy.

He let himself into the house, reached his room and locked the door from within. When he had turned the key in the lock of his door, he paused there for a long time, with his hand on the key, reluctant to light the gas and break the spell that gave his being such happiness. If he lit the gas and, for instance, unlaced his shoes to get into bed, that spell would break and, he felt instinctively, a corresponding unhappiness would follow it. Darkness had suddenly become his natural environment. In darkness, he felt, there was no necessity to think or to act, but to go on for ever being carried on the wind, through the firmament, in ghostly happiness.

He stood with his hand on the key, gently swaying back and forth, with a gentle look in his harassed eyes. He was thinking of nothing. Nothing! It seemed that his brain had worked with feverish energy through all the course of possible human activities, reached the brink of a precipice and hurled itself in despair into an empty abyss.

A slight sound startled him from this mood. It was the crackling of a piece of coal in the dying fire. He jerked forward his chest, inhaled a deep breath through his nostrils and then struck a match. Still holding his nostrils expanded, he went to the gas-jet and lit it. Puff! The light hissed forth yellowishly and then became blue and then white. It filled the room. He drew in another deep breath and then his face wrinkled with anger at the thought that without death it was impossible for ever to contemplate nothing. He sat down on the bed, put his face in his hands and became furiously angry with the force in nature that had doomed him, as a thinking man, to go on and on thinking, trying to reach the end of a road that only led to the brink of a precipice. And he thought of Nietzsche, who had likened himself to a pine tree, swaying over a precipice, hanging on by a single root.

He began to frame articulate sentences in his mind, slowly, arranging each sentence with meticulous care. One which he repeated to himself many times was as follows:

'When a drowning man clutches at a straw, it is symbolical of man's effort to revenge himself on the brutality of nature, by dragging something with him into the abyss of death, and it is also symbolical of man's helplessness.'

After a while he felt a craving for a cigarette. He

was not in the habit of smoking many cigarettes, but now, it seemed that his nerves cried out for tobacco like the nerves of an opium fiend crying for their drug. He lit a cigarette and began to smoke it, inhaling the smoke into his lungs and blowing it out again slowly. His limbs became soft.

A merry thought came into his mind. He said to himself:

'Even better would be, to make a gesture of contempt by informing on the whole business now. As much as to say: "Here. I could kill the fellow if I liked, but nothing is worth while. Have the others instead." '

He pursed up his lips thinking of this. At first he smiled; then the smile changed into a scowl. He chewed the end of his cigarette. Then he crushed it into a pulp between his fingers, turned his head to one side and listened. Now, his face assumed an extraordinary expression. It had a cringing, sly look. It became like the face of an animal, that is slinking around a corner, with a piece of stolen meat between its jaws. His body was rigid, but his eyes moved slowly, from side to side. Then he sprang to his feet, and began to tremble.

A terrible desire took possession of him. He wanted to go out and report at once to the police that arrangements had just been completed for a political assassination of tremendous (yes, he would use the word tremendous) importance. The assassins had arranged to assemble at eleven o'clock on Sunday morning at a given place. And . . .

That thought switched out of his mind, as rapidly as if he had been struck a violent blow on the ear by a man's hand and knocked into a stupor. Instead of it came a terrible fear of death. Now he wanted to hide under the bed and remain there until he became an old man with white hair and toothless jaws; just for the delicious pleasure of being alive and able to think.

On the morrow he would arise, cast away his money and his clothes and present himself at the workhouse gates. They would kindly take him in among the paupers. And he would sit there quietly until old age, thinking; feeling the delicious pleasure of being alive and living quietly without effort, obeying other wills.

Then a voice within him growled and with his own eyes he saw fierce eyes, which he also recognized as his own, staring at him fiercely. He understood in a flash that it was not himself who had been thinking in this cowardly futile manner, but another man. Who? His young manhood, that had been lashed by a shameful sense of inferiority.

He began to strip off his clothes, uttering fierce words. And he now transformed himself into a wild fisherman from his native village, a man without subtle thought to disturb and emasculate his virility, dashing his strength against the barbarous cruelty of nature. He forgot his skinny legs, his sunken eyes, his pallid, nervous cheeks, the softness of his muscles, and he felt himself towering over the angry sea in a boat, with god-like power, yelling defiance at the gale. He saw, from the rock-bound coast, civilized man afar off and spat at him with contempt.

He paused when he had stripped himself to his underwear and stood still, rubbing his hands over his chest. He thought:

'She said I was a half-savage from the wilds of Kerry.'

His mouth opened wide. His fury left him and he became sad. Gradually, his lips closed again, his face shut up, his eyes became locked doors concealing his mind. Once more, he stood aloft, looking down with equanimity on life, on his sordid birth, on his youth, when he had been drawn away from primitive, peasant thoughtlessness by a thirst for knowledge, on his young manhood, when the primitive man in him, timid in its strange atmosphere of complex thought, grew morbid with a sense of inferiority and injustice, onwards towards the chaos of unbelief. Ha! He had climbed to a height and now he could look down.

'In one stroke,' he said aloud, in a whisper, 'I'll free myself.'

He raised his right forefinger, as if explaining a statement to somebody. He smiled in a strange manner, raising upwards the right side of his mouth. He winked his right eye and whispered gently:

'That's it. Now I have it.'

Then he grew calm and got into bed. He fell asleep at once. While he slept there was a smile on his countenance. He dreamt all night of his mother.

CHAPTER FOURTEEN

NEXT morning he left the house before nine o'clock. He went to Nelson Pillar and there he boarded a Dalkey tram-car. He entered a post office when he reached Dalkey and dispatched the following telegram to himself, under his assumed name of Carter:

'Report Monday morning, eleven, Captain Pritchard, Liverpool. Johnson.'

After dispatching the telegram, he went into a public-house and sat for a while over a bottle of stout. Then he boarded another tram-car and came back to Dublin. It was twelve o'clock when he returned to his lodgings. He met the servant in the hall and she told him excitedly that the landlady had a telegram for him.

'Ha!' he said. 'I was expecting that.'

He went into the kitchen. The landlady handed him the telegram in silence. He opened it at once.

'Hurrah!' he said, when he had glanced over it hurriedly. 'I've got the job. It means going to sea again, but I'm getting a job as a steward now. That won't be so bad.'

He handed the telegram to the landlady.

'Look,' he said.

The landlady read the telegram, holding it out far from her eyes. She handed it back and said in a low voice:

'I'll be sorry to lose ye.'

He took her hand in both of his and pressed it. Then he said fervently:

'It's not always what we want in life that we get, Mrs. Buggy, and . . . in a way . . . maybe there is some power watching over us . . . sending us here and there, unknown to ourselves, out of harm.'

The landlady looked at him suspiciously and he thought:

'Blast it! that was wrong. She might get suspicious.'

So he began to press her hand and assumed a melancholy, confused expression. The look of suspicion left her face and she said:

'Ah! Go on outa that. Yer too serious entirely. Yer only a boy. That'll be all right. Seeing as yer an ex-service man, I'll let ye have back the remainder . . .'

'Oh! No, Mrs. Buggy,' he said hurriedly. 'Not at all. That wouldn't be fair. I'm not short. I'm not the kind of man who goes in for foolishly spending his money, but I keep my bargain. You'll return nothing. The only thing I'm sorry for is that I have to leave your kind house so hurriedly.'

'You're a nice boy,' she said, pinching his cheek. 'Will ye be going to-morrow or this evening?'

'This evening,' he said. 'I'll have to go this evening, to arrange about kit in Liverpool. We might sail on Monday, you know.'

CHAPTER FIFTEEN

He left the landlady and went to his room to pack his belongings. Then he got into a panic.

'What on earth am I to do with these two suitcases?' he thought, rubbing his hands through his hair.

He had made no provision in his plan for this minute detail and he was utterly at a loss. For it became apparent to him that he was incapable of forming any plan other than what had been organized by his mind before he arrived in Dublin. Supposing, then, that any unforeseen event happened, necessitating a change in the other arrangements?

'God!' he muttered. 'What am I to do with these things? If I leave them here, the landlady will become suspicious. If I move through the town carrying them, I'll attract attention. What am I to do with them?'

He sat down and put his head in his hands, thinking. After a while he jumped to his feet and clapped his hands together:

'I have it,' he cried. 'The pawn office.'

He locked the door and stripped himself naked. From the large suitcase, he took the new clothes that he had kept hidden until then. He put them on. When he had finished dressing, he examined himself in the looking-glass. He straightened his shoulders and smiled. He nodded his head at his own reflection.

'That's good,' he said to himself. 'See what a change clothes make and the absence of that stoop! God! I'll be glad when I can straighten myself again.'

Now he looked a fashionable young man and rather handsome, dressed in a light brown suit, with a light blue shirt and collar. Having examined himself carefully, to see that everything was all right, he put his socks outside his trouser legs and then pulled on his old trousers over the new ones. He put on his new overcoat. Then he pulled on his loose raincoat.

'Do I look too fat now, though?' he thought nervously.

He looked in the mirror. He did look slightly too fat, but not very noticeably. He decided that nobody would notice it and the landlady would believe that he had put on more clothes to guard against cold during the sea voyage. He was satisfied and slightly thrilled at the solving of his difficulty in this easy manner. He packed all his clothes into the small suitcase and then put the small suitcase into the larger one. He was about to lock the large one, when he started and thought:

'Hello! What about my old coat and waistcoat?'

He hurriedly opened the small suitcase again, rummaged about and got his old coat and waistcoat. He held them in his right hand for a long time, nervously wondering what to do with them.

'Curse it, I can't put them all on. Wait a moment.

I must wrap them up. They won't make a big parcel. Hold on, though. Yes, I have it. I'll be wearing my overcoat. I won't need the new coat and waistcoat.'

He took off both overcoats again. Then he took off his new coat and waistcoat. He put on the old ones. He put on the new overcoat. He went to the mirror to see did the old coat and waistcoat show beneath the new overcoat. They did not. He was satisfied and sighed with relief. Again, he put on his loose raincoat and buttoned it carefully about his throat. He put on his shabby cap and examined himself in the mirror.

'God!' he said. 'Am I mad or what? I can't wear this old cap. Where is that hat? And the handkerchief too. Every little thing counts.'

He took the hat and the coloured handkerchief from the suitcase. He stuffed both into the pocket of his new overcoat, under the raincoat. Then he arranged the suitcases as before, one within the other.

Then he bid good-bye to the landlady, telling her that he had to go out to Dalkey to see Colonel Johnson before leaving Dublin. Carrying his suitcase in his hand, he set off for Marlborough Street, in order to pawn the suitcase and its contents.

The clerk accepted the pledge.

CHAPTER SIXTEEN

IT was three o'clock when he left the pawn office. He felt very elated. Having got rid of his suitcases and of his landlady, it appeared to him that the most important part of the business was done. The rest appeared simple. The assassination itself did not enter his mind at all. He was now merely concerned with working out the details of his plan. And he felt at peace with life, just like a business man who has just put through a profitable deal and is reflecting that society is marvellously well arranged for the purpose of providing happiness for deserving citizens.

He rubbed his palms together and thought of having a meal. So he went and ate a huge beef-steak in a workman's restaurant. He took his time with the meal and devoured every morsel. He felt very strong, warm and comfortable. He left the restaurant in excellent spirits, almost intoxicated with the pleasure of having feasted well.

Then, suddenly, he started and thought:

'Heavens above! Supposing she refuses to leave after all! God only knows what a crazy person like that could be capable of doing.'

He thrust out his lower lip, frowned and said to himself that he would make her leave, and quickly too. He was now in a vulgar, smug mood, exactly like a stockbroker whose business is thriving. Everything appeared simple and arranged for his express satisfaction. Even the weather had improved. The streets were dry. The sun shone, not very brightly, but with the soft warmth of approaching summer. As he walked along, in this mood, he felt like nodding to the policemen on duty and calling out to them:

'That's right, me lads. Keep good order in this town. Keep the wheels running smoothly.'

He went into a billiard room and loafed there for an hour watching the games, with great interest, perfectly at peace. Then, at six o'clock, he went towards Capel Street, to keep his appointment with Kitty Mellett. He went slowly, although the appointment was for six o'clock and it was now some minutes after six. But this mood made him indifferent as to whether he was ten minutes or an hour late.

'Let her wait,' he thought. 'I'm in control of the situation. This is a very simple business.'

In fact, at the southern entrance to Capel Street, he paused for some time, listening to a policeman who was arguing with a carter. The carter was trying to get an enormous dray out of the way of the traffic. The dray was drawn across the street and the two horses were rearing up, terrified by the headlights of a tram-car that was just in front of them. The carter was pointing at the tram-conductor with his upraised whip and the policeman was saying, with his notebook in his hand:

'That'll do you now. Tell that to the magistrate.'

McDara looked on, laughing, with his hands in

173

his pockets. Suddenly the carter moved off, cursing loudly and lashing his horses. The policeman, waving his arms, began to shout to the crowd that had gathered:

'Move on there now.'

'Good heavens!' exclaimed McDara.

He darted up Capel Street at a furious pace. The policeman's voice had changed his mood. The policeman had approached him, striding, with his arms raised, and there was an angry look on his face.

McDara almost ran up Capel Street, thinking the policeman was after him. A new, hitherto unexperienced terror took possession of him. He thought that he had gone mad and that this whole plan had been suggested to him by a Government agent, whom he had forgotten. He thought that the secret police were using him without his being aware of it; that they would allow everything to proceed until the hour of the assassination; then they would seize him, grin, twist his arms and frog-march him to the lunatic asylum.

He was perspiring when he arrived at the corner of the lane, where he was to meet Kitty. She was there in the doorway. Careless of attracting attention, he rushed up to her and caught her by the arms.

'Is that you, Kitty?' he murmured excitedly. 'I was afraid I'd lose you. I got into an awful state. I . . .'

Then he swallowed his breath, paused and looked at her, with a dazed look in his eyes. She also looked

174

terrified. She was pale. The dark rings under her grey eyes were more apparent. Her face was now entirely without charm. It looked old. Her hands toyed with an umbrella. She was wearing a belted brown overcoat, that looked very clumsy on her. Her hat, too, was ugly, a piece of black cloth, of an uncouth shape.

'I got terrified too,' she said, 'waiting here. I thought you weren't coming and that something had happened.'

Her ugliness calmed him. And, with the curious inconsistency of the human mind, he thought, as he looked at her:

'What on earth did I ever see in her?'

Then he looked at her tenderly and clasped her hand.

'Kitty,' he said, 'you've been a real friend to me.'

For some reason, her ugliness had aroused a tender emotion in him, which her beauty had never aroused.

'Michael,' she whispered, clutching at his breast, 'you won't let me down, will you?'

'Have no fear,' he whispered earnestly, sincerely.

She spoke in a subdued tone, looking up at him, with love in her eyes.

'I'm going,' she continued. 'I've left my things at the station. You see, I have obeyed you in everything.'

'Kitty,' he began, and then he paused, not knowing what to say.

'I know it's best,' she said. 'Even before you came I had thought of going. I had become so tired of this country. And of my life. There is nothing left here. And even what you are going to do . . . that will not mean what I thought it would. It won't be a human act but the hand of God reaching out in vengeance for our crimes. For all our crimes. It won't be an awakening but the final act in a terrible tragedy. I can see that. And . . . I'm finished. You won't desert me, though, will you?'

McDara kept pressing her hand and nodding his head. He was not listening to what she said, but a cloud of dark passion surged through his body and he looked upon the morrow's corpse with brutal joy. It appeared magnificent to his mind.

'I don't want you to live with me,' she continued. 'But . . . I feel you have ideas about life that might be . . . I do. I do. I do want to have you with me. You won't leave me, will you? This will change everything. I could never come back again. We are all getting old and we're all like empty bottles, out of which the wine has been drunk. The ideals we started life with broken and shattered. Can't you see it? This is the end, not the beginning. There will be no result from this but . . . It will be like a drug silencing the murmurs of the disillusioned.'

'Who's that man standing over there?' said Mc-Dara.

She started and looked across the street. There was a tall man standing there, lighting his pipe. He threw the match away, pressed his forefinger into the glowing bowl and passed on.

'It's nobody,' she said listlessly.

He looked up and down the street.

'It's very bright here,' he said. 'I wonder are we being watched?'

'No,' she said slowly. 'Nobody will watch. And even if they do they can't see. This is fate.'

He let go her hand, which he had been holding and pressing until then. He had suddenly become bored with her. His face grew angry.

'You'll go by the mail boat this evening?' he said.

'Yes,' she said.

'You won't forget where you're to meet me in London?'

'No,' she said. 'I won't forget.'

'Tell me, though. Does your mother know you're going?'

'Yes. She's only too glad. I told her I was going to see my sister. I have a sister living at Putney.'

'Oh! Have you, though? That's good.'

'How do you mean?' she said sharply.

'Eh?' he said dreamily, as if he had not been listening to her. 'Why? What did I say? I was just thinking.'

'No. No. Tell me. You're not going to leave me in London. You won't send me off to my sister's?'

She began to shed tears and mumbled:

'I'm so ashamed. I feel as weak and cowardly as a child.'

McDara folded his arms and looked at the ground.

'You seem to forget,' he said, 'that I might never reach London.'

'How do you mean?'

'Eh?' he said. 'I might be a corpse before to-morrow night. Anything may happen.'

She began to shudder. Then she wiped her eyes.

'Have you got enough money to do you?' said McDara.

'Listen,' she said, in an awed whisper. 'Don't do it, Michael. Come away with me now. Let somebody else do it.'

'H'm!' said McDara.

'They're no use,' he thought. 'They're just a bag of nerves. How on earth did I ever have any interest in these mystical lunatics?'

'Do you hear me?' she continued. 'Don't do it.'

There was no force or fervour in her voice. She seemed utterly helpless and exhausted. Her eyes were bloodshot. Her lips hung loose. They quivered.

'Now, Kitty,' he said quietly. 'Don't make me feel ashamed of you.'

'Oh!' she said in a frightened tone. 'What did I say? I don't know what I'm saying. I didn't say good-bye to Kathleen or to Sheila. Don't think I was foolish in any way. I've never said a word to anybody, only to mother, and I just told her I was going over to Marjorie, to ask for a job or something. I've often been away, you know. My mother is not a bit interested, you know. I tell you I haven't been near Kathleen or any of the others since. As a matter of fact, I avoided Nora Cook in the street this morning for fear she'd . . .'

'Now, look here,' said McDara, taking her firmly by the arm. 'Do you feel fit for this journey?'

'Yes, yes,' she said hurriedly. 'I'm all right.'

'Well, then, cheer up. Don't make me feel nervous too. I have work to do.'

'All right,' she whispered, almost inaudibly. 'I'll go.'

'Take care of yourself,' he said quietly.

She raised her head, puckered up her lips and then whispered:

'Kiss me, Michael.'

McDara looked about him and then hurriedly touched her lips with his. She leaned against his chest and shivered.

'You won't forget now,' she said excitedly. 'You won't desert me.'

'I never break my word,' he muttered. 'That is . . . unless I'm dead, or snatched.'

'You won't, you won't,' she whispered. 'It's fate. That's why I'm . . . I'm upset. It's the end for all of us. There's going to be no God after this. Good-bye.'

She hurriedly pressed his hand and walked away.

CHAPTER SEVENTEEN

Her departure thrilled him. Although he had been bored by her presence and irritated by her whining words, when she moved away and became small, diminishing in the distance, he felt that a deep chord in his consciousness had been touched. A wild longing possessed him, not for her, but for something indefinite, connected with his youth. Proudly, he saw the figure of his mother, standing with her arms folded and her loving eyes flooded with tears, while he was carried away in a train, tearless. He saw the people of his youth, rising up and dancing to the twanging of a bow on a fiddle, leaping in a barbaric dance and shouting wild words to the music. He saw mountainous waves, belching their foam against cliffs, with thunderous sounds. He saw horses galloping in a gale, with widespread nostrils. He saw towering mountains, with eagles sitting on their peaks, among the snow and ice.

All this panorama, of wild earth and sea and man and animal, became, in his imagination, a single gesture of furious longing and revolt, a sudden, powerful heaving up towards the expression of something eternal and majestic. As if all life and movement had united in one effort to abolish death and weakness and create an unchanging eternity of force; and of beauty through force.

He absorbed this force into his being and felt himself powerfully strong and cool, the embodiment of the

whole power of the universe. The ecstasy of limitless pride possessed him, an ecstasy far greater than
that of the greatest love, because there was no softness
in it; it was of one substance, without enervating
heat, without desire, without any of the properties that
mar happiness by causing a desire for ravishment.

He moved away towards Tumulty's room. It
was not yet seven o'clock. He was not due there
until nine. But he was not really moving towards
Tumulty's room, for the purpose of meeting
Tumulty and Fetch. He was performing a movement on an interior plane, the plane of his inner
consciousness, towards the spot where he was to
strike the blow. He was now closely united to the
being of HIM, who was doomed to die. HE, according to McDara's mind, was also moving slowly,
driven by another inscrutable force, in a circular
route, towards the spot where he was to collide with
McDara's will and die.

McDara saw HIM clearly, moving, in a circular
route, with the sombre movements of a person en-
tranced, advancing towards the spot. And now, there
was no passion in McDara's mind with regard to
HIM. HE, as it were, had become a part of McDara.
They had become two parts of one whole. The more
powerful part would survive.

He threw back his head and his neck became stiff
when his mind recorded this fact, that the more powerful part would survive. A ringing voice exclaimed
within him: 'Then my power 'll be unfathomable.'

He walked instinctively until he reached the slum street where Tumulty had his secret room. He entered the open door of the gloomy house and began to mount the stairs. Half-way up the stairs, he heard the patter of light feet coming towards him from above. Then a match was struck. It lit, flickered and went out. He ascended slowly. The feet came nearer. Another match was struck. It flared up dimly, just above him, on the stairs. He raised his head. A young woman stood above him. He paused and looked at her. She also stood, holding the lighted match in front of her face.

He saw at once that she was a harlot, by the harlot's stare in her damned eyes. He passed her. She moved downwards, striking matches to light her way, lest she might soil her market finery by contact with the foul walls or banisters. She was the harlot who occupied the room opposite Tumulty's room.

He arrived at the door of Tumulty's room and stood there with his hands in his pockets, staring at the bottom of the door, like a dog waiting for admission. No light peered from the bottom of the door. There was deadly silence on the landing. It was nearly pitch-dark, except for a faint gleam of light that came through a tiny window in the far wall over the hollow of the stairway.

He made no movement either to knock or to look about him. He stood there, staring at the bottom of the door, with his mind fixed on the union of his

personality with that of the man who was doomed
to die.

Then he grew worried, because his imagination
absolutely refused to advance farther than the spot
where the two personalities joined and became one.

With that, he stood erect and folded his arms on
his chest. He turned slightly to his left and stared
at the tiny window, through which the dim light was
creeping. His body became fixed in that attitude.
His mind, instead of advancing boldly beyond the
slain body of his enemy, gazed backwards at the wild
men, who were dancing with savage tumult to the
twanging of a bow on a fiddle. Everything became
chaotic, senseless, without purpose. His skull seemed
to fill with fiery particles, that rushed about burning
the mechanism of his reason. He now wanted to
laugh aloud, the hysterical laughter of defeat. He
saw himself being stripped naked by these wild men
and turned loose in a wilderness of barren rocks.

His mind began to wander foolishly, very hurriedly, creating a disgusting life for this naked man,
amid scenes of lust and degradation. He stood
limply, with his eyes almost closed and his lower lip
thrust out, like a drunken man.

Then he heard Tumulty coming up the stairs. He
began to walk about the landing, rubbing his hands
together and saying to himself with great glee:
'This is great. This is great.' Tumulty stopped
several times coming up the stairs, suspicious of the
steps that were pattering about the landing. Then

he came up the last flight at a run and whispered sharply:

'Who's there?'

McDara answered him. Tumulty, without replying, hurriedly unlocked the door and entered the room. He had a parcel under his arm. McDara followed him into the room.

'Where is Fetch?' said McDara.

'He'll be along in a moment,' said Tumulty irritably. 'We didn't want to come in together, blast it. Wait. I wonder is that tart in her room? What in the name o' God were ye walkin' around the landing for?'

'Don't worry,' said McDara. 'I saw her going out as I was coming up. Light the lamp.'

Tumulty gripped McDara by the arm and said excitedly:

'Did she see ye? Did she speak?'

'Hush, hush,' said McDara. 'Don't lose yer head, man. Is the car all right?'

Tumulty remained silent for a moment and then he whispered, in a sibilant voice, through his teeth:

'The car is all right.'

'Come, light the lamp,' said McDara sharply.

He wanted to see Tumulty's face. He did not like the sound of Tumulty's voice.

'Wait till I bring in Fetch,' said Tumulty. 'He doesn't know the way. You light the lamp. Put a blanket over the window first.'

He went out, leaving the door open. McDara

184

took the quilt off the bed, mounted a chair and covered the window with the quilt. Then he struck a match. He lit the lamp that hung on a nail in the wall. He looked about the room. There was food there now, laid on a newspaper by the wall near the fire. The fire was set in the grate. Beside the food, laid on a newspaper, there was a long bottle, wrapped in brown paper, tied with twine.

'Ha!' said McDara to himself. 'Fetch is cool. He has thought of that.'

He listened. They were coming up. They entered the room, stepping lightly. Fetch was grinning. He struck his gloved hands together when he caught sight of McDara. He winked his right eye.

'She's on,' he whispered. 'The bus is a dandy. She'll travel like forked lightning. You watch.'

Tumulty locked the door carefully and left the key in the lock. The three men came up to the fire and stood there in silence for several moments, looking at one another. They seemed to be waiting for something.

'Here, light this fire,' said Tumulty.

'Lemme do it,' said Fetch.

He went on his knees. McDara looked anxiously at Tumulty. He scratched his head under his cap.

'You look all right, Frank,' he said. 'That'll go all right, I think. Turn round.'

Tumulty was dressed in plus-fours and a belted raincoat. He wore a new brown hat. The red tabs on his stockings showed beneath the rim of the rain-coat. But his face looked incongruous, for some reason, in this attire. He looked ferocious and un-balanced. His puffy cheeks were pale. His neck was swollen. He did not turn round when McDara told him to do so, but said angrily:

'What the hell is the idea? This is not a tailor's shop.'

'Damn it, man!' said McDara.

Fetch looked up from the fire and said to Tumulty:
'Open that bottle, Frank, and have a swig.'

Tumulty went over to the bottle. He laid down the parcel he had under his arm and then picked it up again. Fetch winked at McDara seriously.

'Ye know what,' said Tumulty, suddenly break-ing into a low, hoarse, gurgling peal of laughter. 'It's this bloomin' parcel.'

He held out the parcel.

'What?' said McDara.

'Honest to God!' said Tumulty. 'I carried this with me from the house and it put the wind up me.'

'Have a drink, man,' said Fetch, striking a match.

'What's in it?' said McDara.

'Only me old clothes,' said Tumulty, with sudden gaiety, pitching the parcel on to the bed. 'Me trousers an' cap. O' course I should have brought the other kit here instead, but I got all messed up. What is it? White Horse be the holy!'

He held up the bottle. McDara sat down,

186

'Is the car all right, then?' he said to Fetch.

'Sure,' said Fetch. 'Hey, Frank, that's a funny joker, that Rummel. His name isn't really Rummel, is it?'

'What Rummel?' said McDara, looking from one to the other of them.

'One o' my men,' said Tumulty, uncorking the bottle with a popping sound. 'No. His name isn't Rummel.'

'A live wire,' said Fetch, getting to his feet. 'Good fellah that. That's a bright lot o' fellahs you've got, Frank, by all accounts.'

Tumulty and Fetch sat down side by side on the bed, talking to one another with enthusiastic friendliness. They seemed to take no notice of McDara and to treat him as if he were of no consequence. McDara became excited and very angry.

'Don't drink too much of that whisky,' he said sharply.

They both looked at him sourly.

'Have ye got that weapon for me?' he said to Tumulty.

'Plenty o' time,' said Tumulty. 'What's the hurry? We've all night to settle that. Don't get excited, man.'

McDara got to his feet and came over to the bed. He snatched the bottle from Tumulty's hand. His face became savage.

'Listen, you two,' he muttered.

They sat still, looking at him.

187

'I'm in command of this job,' he said quietly. 'No monkey tricks. What have you got up yer sleeve, Frank?'

Tumulty jumped up. His throat quivered. He stooped forward.

'What schemes have you been concocting with Gutty to-day?' said McDara. 'Out with it.'

Tumulty licked his upper lip with his lower lip. Then he folded his arms, leaned forward from his hips and said through his teeth:

'You're in command until this job is done. Then I'm in command.'

He tapped his chest and added:

'Afterwards.'

McDara's lips grew pale. Then he smiled. He looked at Fetch. Fetch was leaning forward on the bed, with his head stooping and his cunning eyes darting from one to the other rapidly. The scar on his cheek had again become white.

'That's an old gag of yours, Gutty, isn't it?' said McDara.

Fetch did not speak. Tumulty swelled out his chest.

'What are ye drivin' at now?' he said to McDara.

'Sit down,' said McDara angrily. 'I know all about it. But you're not going to do it. Dye hear?'

'Who's to prevent me?' snapped Tumulty.

'Very well, then,' said McDara rapidly. 'What do you intend doing?'

Tumulty leaned forward and whispered tensely:

'I'm goin' to carry on afterwards.'

'In what way?'

Tumulty tapped McDara on the chest and whispered:

'In twenty-four hours after the job is done this town is goin' to be in the middle of a revolution.'

McDara smiled broadly and moved towards the fire with the bottle. Tumulty followed him. Fetch still sat on the bed, with his head stuck forward. His eyes gleamed now.

'So you wanted to clear out like a rabbit and leave us in the mush?' said Tumulty. 'But we're not in this for the purpose of makin' an experiment for any o' your bum theories. We're in this for the purpose o' bringin' off a revolution. See?'

McDara sat down on a chair by the fire. He was still smiling.

'Yes,' he said, nodding towards Fetch. 'That's an old gag o' yours, Gutty.'

'Speak to me,' said Tumulty angrily. 'Don't mind Gutty.'

McDara uttered a foul oath and put the bottle on the floor.

'Just like two women,' he muttered.

'By Christ!' said Tumulty.

'Yes,' said McDara, looking up suddenly at Tumulty. 'We'll see who'll be the rabbit after the job is done. We'll see.'

'Yes, you will see,' said Tumulty.

They stared at one another. Fetch slid off the bed

and approached them, walking like a jockey. His lips trembled.

'Let up on it,' he muttered, standing in front of them. 'Have you fellahs got no gumption?'

They both looked at him. Fetch looked terrifying. His dark face, with the little cunning eyes and the whitish scar, had a ghoulish appearance.

'I can't talk,' he said. 'But I can fight. That's all. Well then, let's fight. Not cut an' run. Let's go on fightin' till we drop. Know what I mean? 'Slong as I'm fightin' . . . 'sall right. Take 'em as they come. Then every man 'sequal. Die that way. That's m'idea. Savvy? There's no gag in this, Mac. 'Selp me God.'

Then he began to shake all over.

'I want to put mesel' right,' he added in a whisper.

There was a tense silence.

'Who's going to make the revolution?' said McDara suddenly.

Tumulty knelt on one knee beside McDara.

'I've got ten men,' he said excitedly.

McDara looked at him with bloodshot eyes.

'Ten men,' he said wearily.

'Don't ye see?' said Tumulty, tapping the tips of the fingers of his left hand with the tip of the forefinger of his right hand. 'Instead of lying low or cutting out after the job is done, we wait until the fury o' the mob is at fever pitch. . . .'

McDara smiled and said:

'That's a good phrase.'

'Then we walk in,' continued Tumulty, 'an' crease an important Republican. They'll think it's a reprisal. So, the game is let loose. Nothing can stop it then.'

'Then an archbishop or a couple o' priests,' said Fetch.

'It's up in a blaze,' said Tumulty. 'I got ten men that'll go through hell's fire. There'd be a thousand men in an hour. Man, man, there are thousands waiting ready to rush out, waitin' for their chance.'

'To loot,' said McDara calmly. 'That's not force. There's no reason in that. That's mob anarchy. There's no purpose behind. Oh! Here,' he cried, jumping to his feet. 'Do you think I'M afraid?'

He paused. His face contorted. His sunken eyes blazed. They drew back.

'If you can show me anything that I believe is good I'll do it. But I'm not an Irishman. I'm simply a man.'

'Steady now,' said Tumulty.

'Dig in with us,' said Fetch. 'You turned the proposition down in New York. So I let it go. But Frank an' I had a talk to-day. An' it seems we both had the same idea. So . . . we're goin' ahead. Dig in with us, Mac. You got the brains.'

'Easy now, easy now,' said Tumulty, waving aside Fetch with his hand. 'There's brains enough on this job. Don't you forget it. Let him come in if he likes. If he doesn't, let him step aside. He can cut out as soon as his own plan is carried out. That's all.'

McDara began to rub his hands together slowly.

'Go on, boys,' he said suddenly. 'Drink away. Have a drink. Have a drink.'

He began to smile again, straight into their faces. They both looked at him in amazement. He wagged his head and said:

'Don't forget that now, Frank,' he said. 'We'll see who is the rabbit after the job is done. You take command afterwards. I'm agreed. I'll obey you. That'll be splendid. But don't forget. I'm going to ask you that question. Who's the rabbit now? I'm going to ask you that. You don't know how I'll enjoy having the responsibility of command thrust on to you. Go ahead now. Have a drink. Let's be jolly. Eat, sleep and be merry, for to-morrow we die. Let's get into that state to keep our trigger fingers cool. You drink. I'll tell stories. Let's be merry. Sit down. Sit down. Don't stand there, like two rabbits. Come on, boys, look cheerful. Everything is now prepared. There's no more to be done. Let's enjoy ourselves.'

They still looked at him in amazement.

'What are ye gaping at?' he continued. 'I'm not fooling. What I said goes. After this job is done, I resign command and place myself at the disposal of Frank Tumulty for the purpose of carrying out a revolution. I'll take his orders. That's agreed. I'm no rabbit.'

Tumulty still stared in amazement. Fetch stood very erect, looked at McDara ferociously and then stepped towards the bottle.

'Blast this story!' he said.

He picked up the bottle and put it to his head.

'Hey, Mac,' said Tumulty, raising his hand.

Suddenly McDara opened his eyes wide and whispered:

'Listen.'

They all stood still, listening. Footsteps were coming up the stairs to the top landing. Tumulty reached the lamp in two bounds and blew it out. Fetch put down the bottle in silence and drew his pistol from his bosom. McDara approached Tumulty, walking on his toes. He groped for Tumulty in the darkness and whispered:

'Hand over that gat.'

Tumulty handed out a revolver. McDara cocked it. Then the three of them stood still, with their weapons in their hands, listening. They distinguished the footsteps. There were two people walking up. One walked lightly in front. The other staggered heavily behind. Tumulty whispered through his teeth:

'It's the tart and a man.'

'She saw me,' whispered McDara; 'would the man be a tout?'

'No,' said Tumulty. 'She wouldn't come in that case.'

'Hush.'

'Is there no end to these stairs?' said a hoarse, drunken voice.

'Don't talk so loud,' said a woman's voice. 'We're at the top now. Steady on.'

'What did I tell ye?' whispered Tumulty. 'She's just got a man.'

They heard the door of the harlot's room being opened.

'Come on, dearie,' she said.

The door was shut.

'Who's that?' said Fetch.

Tumulty and McDara went on tiptoe to the fire.

'It's a tart gone into the other room with a man,' he said to Fetch.

'Eh?' said Fetch.

'Damn that!' said McDara. 'Will he stay the night?'

'Don't think so,' said Tumulty. 'He'll only stay for a short time. She never keeps men here for the night.'

'Hell of a story,' said Fetch.

'Hush, hush,' said McDara. 'Keep quiet here. We better leave the light out.'

They sat around the fire for a long time, in silence, listening excitedly. Their eyes kept wandering towards the door. There was perfect silence.

Then again they started, hearing footsteps on the stairs.

'Great God Almighty!' whispered Tumulty. 'D'ye hear that?'

Steps were coming up stealthily. They all got to their feet.

'Touts,' hissed McDara. 'We're spotted. Stand ready. Give it to them. Give us more ammunition, Frank.'

They spread out over the floor, ready to make a fight for their lives. Then there was a rush of feet on the landing.

'Open that door,' shouted a gruff voice.

Then they heard fists hammering on the harlot's door.

McDara moved over to Tumulty and whispered:

'It's a raid on the . . .'

'Hist!' said Tumulty.

'Open, open,' shouted the voice.

'Give it a shoulder,' said another voice.

The woman screamed.

'Come out here. Who are you? What are you doin' here? Answer. What's yer name?'

There was a tumult of voices. Then they heard:

'Let me go. I'm a woman, anyway. Josephine Scully, I say. Don't touch me.'

A voice on the landing said gruffly:

'You proceed homewards now.'

'Listen, constable, I want to speak to ye a moment.'

'Proceed homewards now. That'll do.'

'What's he whisperin' to ye there?'

'That's she right enough. Hey, my girl, do ye know anything about a hundred an' ten quid was pinched in Stephen's Green th'other day? Wha'?

Ye catch an unfortunate man up from the country
. . .'

'That's a lie. I didn't take it.'

'That'll do ye now. Come quietly. The woman is
rotten.'

'Hey. Hold on. Who lives here? Who lives in
this room?'

McDara touched Tumulty's arm. Fetch went on
one knee. He put the tips of his fingers on the
ground, like a man waiting to begin a race. Somebody rattled the door-knob.

'Who?'

'I don't know. Nobody, I think.'

The door-knob was shaken again.

'Anybody in there?'

'Come on away. It's unoccupied.'

'Eh?'

'Come on, man.'

The door-knob was shaken again. Then the voices
and the footsteps began to go downstairs.

Fetch stood up.

'Is there a lavatory on this landing?' he said.

'Stand still a moment,' McDara said.

They remained silent for a minute or more. Then
Tumulty went to the window. He raised a corner
of the bedspread and peered out. Then he came back
on tiptoe.

'They're takin' her up the road,' he said.

'What time is it?' said McDara.

Nobody replied.

'Gimme a drink,' said Tumulty, after a pause.

They all had a swig at the bottle.

'Better leave the lamp out,' said McDara.

'All right,' said Tumulty.

'I know,' said Fetch.

He moved towards the door.

'Where are ye goin'?' they both said.

'All right,' he muttered. 'I'll be back in a moment.'

He unlocked the door and went out. McDara crouched over the fire and lit a cigarette. Tumulty knelt by the fire and put his hands to the blaze.

'Did ye ever read about Rasputin, the Russian monk?' he said in a whisper to McDara.

McDara grunted.

'Want a fag?' he said, offering Tumulty an open packet of cigarettes.

Tumulty took one and stroked it between his fingers.

'There was a fellah tryin' to poison him,' he continued, 'but it took no effect. He must have had a constitution like a horse.'

'Ha!' said McDara. 'We better not come back here again . . . to-morrow.'

'Why not?' said Tumulty dreamily.

His face was vacant and his mind was obviously dealing with very distant thoughts . . . about the poisoning of Rasputin.

'Where is the car being taken?' said McDara.

Fetch opened the door and came in. They started

violently. Fetch locked the door and came up to the fire.

'Let's have some grub,' he said.

'No, leave that grub alone,' said Tumulty. 'Maybe we'll want that to-morrow night. We may have to stay here some time. This is the best place.'

'So ye mean to come back here afterwards?' said McDara.

Tumulty looked at McDara and frowned.

'Why not?' he said. 'What's the matter with this place? We'll be well covered by my men.'

'I see,' said McDara.

'Well, if we ain't goin' to eat,' said Fetch gloomily, 'I'm goin' to flop.'

'Hadn't we better go over the details first?' said McDara.

'I'm all right,' said Fetch, taking a blanket off the bed. 'I know my work. You talk it over with Frank if ye want to.'

He laid down on the floor, rolling himself up in the blanket.

'You fellahs can have the bed,' he said.

'I went over the whole thing to-day with Gutty,' whispered Tumulty to McDara. 'Ye see, in the morning . . .'

He whispered rapidly to McDara, explaining how they would leave the room, reach the car and go to the appointed place.

McDara listened in silence, looking into the fire, without thought.

198

When Tumulty had finished, he got to his feet, stretched himself and said:

'I think we had better lie down and try to have a little sleep.'

He went over to the bed. McDara sat still by the fire. Fetch began to mumble to himself. Tumulty laid down on the bed. The bed creaked. Then there was only a sound of breathing. It was still outside. McDara began to shake his head spasmodically. He shut his eyes. Then he raised his eyebrows and expanded his nostrils. He opened his eyes and looked sideways at the recumbent form of Fetch. Fetch was lying on his back with his right knee raised. His mouth was open. He appeared to be asleep.

'What?' said McDara to himself.

'Are you asleep, Gutty?' he whispered.

'Come an' have a lie down,' said Tumulty.

Tumulty was wide awake and his voice was dry. McDara did not reply.

'This is very childish,' he said to himself.

Then he started and turned his head sideways, trying to see within himself the voice that said this. He saw nothing. He had a curious feeling for a moment that his head had fallen off and that he no longer existed.

Then he sighed and clasped his hands together.

'I'm goin' to have a sleep,' said Tumulty.

But his voice was dry and sharp. He was not going to have a sleep. Fetch went on muttering. McDara took out another cigarette and lit it. His hand shook, holding it to his lips. He threw it into the fire.

Then he put his elbows on his knees, put his chin in his palms and stared into the fire. He thought:

'What on earth did I ever see in these two savages?'

The terrible silence became painful.

'It's goin' to be a fine day to-morrow,' said Tumulty, in the same dry, sharp voice.

Fetch sat up, yawned and said:

'Why the hell don't you fellahs go to sleep?'

Nobody answered him. Fetch got up and went to the window. He raised the corner of the bedspread and looked out. Then he took his blanket to another spot and laid down.

'Lie on the bed,' said Tumulty.

Fetch grunted and rolled himself up in the blanket. Tumulty got off the bed and came over to the fire.

'Give us one o' your fags, Mac,' he said.

McDara handed him a cigarette.

'I hate these two fellows,' he thought.

Tumulty sat on his heels, looking into the fire and smoking.

'Any o' you fellahs hear of Jesse James?' said Fetch, raising his head.

'Who was he?' Tumulty said.

Fetch began to talk of Jesse James. He said he met an old man in New York who had been working in a store in a certain town that was attacked by Jesse James.

'He was the best shot that ever lived,' said Fetch. 'This man, James.'

Tumulty finished smoking the cigarette and had a drink out of the bottle. Fetch asked for a drink. He came over to the fire. They all sat around the fire, in silence.

McDara stood up. He took off his shoes and then began to walk around the room.

'What's the idea?' said Tumulty.

'I don't want them to hear me down below,' said McDara.

'But what are ye walkin' about for?' said Tumulty. 'D'ye feel nervous?'

'No,' snapped McDara.

'Leave him alone,' said Fetch to Tumulty.

McDara looked towards Fetch savagely.

'They are low fellows,' he thought. 'I am contaminated.'

He kept walking around the room slowly. Fetch and Tumulty began to tell stories. McDara began to think very calmly and clearly. It became cold, as the fire was dying out and there was no more coal in the room.

McDara began to talk to himself, but without making any sound. His lips moved and he kept rubbing the back of his neck, upwards, against the collar of his coat.

'I have now reached the climax of my dream. I expected to find here a new revelation of life and an explanation of the purpose of my existence. Instead

I find myself in a slum, in a dirty room, in darkness, with two trivial fellows, who have nothing in common with me. I am going to do something which had no meaning and is simply waste of energy. I know that and yet I am going to do it, although it means nothing and it will have no effect, neither for the purpose of explaining my life nor for any other purpose. The whole thing is futile and a gross waste of energy. These men are childish brutes and I also am a childish brute, without any power. So! Well, then! So that is what life is. A childish farce. Ten million ants are not as great as one lion, although they make cities and obey their laws. However . . .'

Hours passed in that way, as they moved about from one corner of the room to another, uttering trivial words and making trivial gestures. They avoided the morrow's work in word and in thought.

The fire went out. Then a streak of light entered the room, around the corner of the hanging quilt.

It was daylight.

CHAPTER EIGHTEEN

Fresh brown gravel had been strewn on the road.
Sparrows were playing with it. They laid on their
breasts, ruffled their feathers, spread their wings and
twirled round and round, uttering continual shrieks.

There was brilliant sunlight. The sky was im-
maculate. To the west, beyond the summit of the
rising road, mountain slopes were visible, afar off.
The mountain slopes glittered. The sun was shining
there on countless streams of white water, that rolled
downwards. The air was so clear, that it was almost
possible to hear the rumbling gurgle of the distant,
white mountain streams.

There were trees on either side of the road. On
the pavement, opposite the playing sparrows, there
was a wooden seat, close against the grey wall of a
little square orchard. The wooden seat was of a
green colour. There were little white spots on it,
where birds had stood. Trees overhung the wall.
They were sprouting. In the sunlight, the sap, ooz-
ing from their pores, glistened. Their buds were
sticky. There was a wild, heavy smell from them.

Opposite the wooden seat, by the far pavement,
there was a small load of gravel, still unstrewn. The
sparrows had made little hollows in it, wallowing.
On that side, there was an iron railing, each rail
shaped like a spear, with a cross-bar, running below
the heads of the spears. The railing was black.
Thick evergreen bushes and yew trees lined the

railing on the inside. Beyond the tops of the bushes
and between the plump bodies of the yew trees, a
distant house was visible. It was of a yellowish
colour.

There was a curve in the iron railing and a gate
in the centre of the curve. The gate led to the distant
yellowish house. The railing of the gate was golden
and black. It glittered in the sunlight. The gate
was closed.

Five yards to the left of the wooden seat, there
was a road leading to the south. Far down that road
there were houses.

The spire of a church rose into the sky to the east
of the yellowish house.

Except for the chattering of the sparrows, there
was complete silence. It was hardly possible to believe that the city stretched to the north. There was
a fog in that direction and dull sounds. But it was
not possible to see the city nor to feel it, except by
looking at the fog in the air, hanging over it. Here,
it looked like the country in spring, with a wild
smell from the sap-oozing trees, with sparrows
chattering on the road, with fresh gravel gleaming
in the sun, with gay streams, flowing in the distance,
down mountain slopes.

The sound of footsteps came from the right. Two
people came walking out of step. One stepped
boldly, striking the ground fiercely, with regular
beats. One could count the seconds, one by one,
with each beat. The other walked irregularly and

scraped the ground with each third or fourth step. The sparrows stopped chattering. Two men appeared around the bend of the road. The sparrows rose, all together, dropping tiny grains of gravel from their brown bodies, to the road. Bobbing up and down, they flew over the trees of the orchard, out of sight.

The two men were McDara and Tumulty. They walked side by side, on the pavement, by the orchard wall, beneath the overhanging trees that cast small branching shadows over them.

Tumulty wore a cap, a belted raincoat and plus-fours. The red tabs on his stockings showed beneath the rim of his raincoat. The calves of his legs looked thick and round. He swung one arm smartly. The other arm was close to his side, with his hand in his bulging pocket. His jaws stuck out. His lips were sucked inwards. His eyes stared dead in front of him.

McDara was dressed in brown, with black shoes. He had a little handkerchief, red with pale stripes in it, in the outside breast-pocket of his overcoat. He walked erect, with his shoulders drawn back far. His pale face was smiling dreamily. His sunken eyes glittered. He kept licking his lower lip with the tip of his tongue.

When they reached the wooden seat, they halted. They looked about them casually. There was nobody in sight. They sat down, side by side. McDara took a packet of cigarettes from his pocket. He offered

one to Tumulty. They both put cigarettes between
their lips. Just as Tumulty was striking a match, the
church bell began to toll. Tumulty dropped the
match to the road. McDara stooped hurriedly and
picked it up before it went out. He lit his cigarette
with it and then dropped it to the road without
offering it to Tumulty. Tumulty reached for Mc-
Dara's lighted cigarette, took it from his lips and lit
his own with it. As he handed it back, McDara
was listening with open mouth to the tolling of the
church bell. Tumulty dug McDara in the side with
his elbow. McDara put out his hand for the cigarette
without looking at it. He caught the cigarette by
the middle, put it to his lips and then spat hurriedly.
He had put the lighted end in his mouth.

They both listened to the tolling of the church
bell. The sound, heavy with melancholy grandeur,
wandered slowly through the sunlit air. One by one,
slowly, at long intervals, the dull sounding peals
boomed, jangled and then died wearily, with a gentle
ring. McDara's mouth was open. His eyelids
lowered over his eyes. One pale hand rested on his
knee. The other hand held the lighted cigarette before his face. The smoke from the cigarette wound
upwards, straight up, in a little curl. Tumulty's
jaws moved slightly in and out, like the belly movements of a panting horse. His arm, above the hand
in his bulging pocket, now stuck out rigidly.

A woman approached from the left. She was leading a little black dog on a leash. She was small and

plump. She wore a grey costume and a black toque. Her skirts just reached to her knees. She walked very erect. Her breasts trembled when she put her left foot to the ground. A tassel that tied her green jumper at her throat swayed slightly between her trembling breasts. Her small, round face moved jerkily from side to side as she chirruped to her dog, pouting her lips.

They watched her with glittering eyes. Tumulty thrust forward his chest. His muscles became taut. He drew up his left leg under the seat. McDara's pale hand moved slowly upwards from his knee and entered beneath his overcoat on his left breast. The fingers closed gently over the cold butt of a revolver.

As she passed, the lady glanced at their legs. The little dog smelt them and strained at the leash. She dragged him away, chirruping with her pouting lips. She passed down the road. They relaxed.

A blackbird, sitting above them in a tree, broke into a wild song. They started. The blackbird flew away, twittering.

They heard the purring of a motor-car to the right. A horn tooted. They touched one another with their elbows. They looked to the right. The purring became louder. Then a dark motor-car appeared around the corner. The sun caught its headlights. They gleamed. Then the body of the car gleamed. It slackened speed as it approached and the purring became very gentle. It passed the wooden seat very slowly on the far side of the road.

The two far wheels passed over the little heap of gravel, causing the car to rise up on that side and shake four times. The driver looked towards them as the car bounced over the heap of gravel. It was Fetch. He was wearing a bowler hat and a dark suit. He winked his left eye as he passed them. Although the scar was on his left cheek, there was now no sign of it. He had rubbed some brown stuff into it. His face was now uniform, dark brown. His lips grinned, but his eyeballs were slightly distended. His right hand grasped the wheel so violently that the glove had moved up from the wrist, exposing the wrist below the cuff of his coat. There were dark hairs on the wrist.

Neither of them saluted him. Neither did they make any sign in answer to his wink. The car moved slowly until it had passed the gate. Then it halted, a little beyond the mouth of the road that passed downwards to the left of the wooden seat. He turned off the engine and leaned back in his seat, rummaging among his clothes. He took out a packet of cigarettes and lit one.

The bell had now ceased to toll. The three men remained perfectly still, with cigarettes in their hands, listening. The eyes of McDara and of Tumulty were fixed on the lighted cigarette in Fetch's hand. Fetch's eyes stared down the road that led southwards to the left of the wooden seat. Their eyes did not blink. The skin around their eyes gradually strained, until it became very white.

Then they all started and glanced hurriedly to the east. There were slack steps coming from that direction. Other steps came from the west. They glanced in that direction also. Their bodies made slight convulsive movements. McDara's eyes sought the eyes of Tumulty and of Fetch, rapidly, going from one pair to the other in rapid succession. Now his eyes gleamed fiercely. There was the fixed stare of insanity in them. They warned. They spoke. They shot fire. The other eyes relaxed and quivered under their fierce glare. Then McDara's eyes also relaxed. But his hand crept again into the left breast pocket of his overcoat. His fingers closed on the butt of a revolver. Tumulty's arm was rigid. Fetch opened his lips outwards, like a baby about to kiss. He pushed his bowler hat back from his forehead.

From the west, a large woman came walking rapidly. She was dressed in blue. She carried a walking-stick. She kept clearing her throat. There were pouches under her eyes. Her nose was red. Her cheeks were speckled with reddish spots on a yellowish surface. They looked away from her to the east. A sorry-looking person had appeared on that side. He was an old man, who kept scratching his shoulders against his clothes as he walked. He was wearing a white overall, like a medical student. He had a stick in his right hand, held in front of him like a staff. Now and again, he prodded things on the road with the staff and he stooped once to pick up a cigarette butt. They could see his face disfigured by lupus. Under the overall he wore a shaggy, torn, black overcoat.

The woman passed them first, walking at a rapid pace. She looked at each of them as she passed, apparently with interest. But her eyes looked with equal interest at the grey wall of the orchard, at the budding trees and at a seagull that was flying high overhead, going towards the sea. When she passed the old man, he raised aloft his stick, saluting.

The old man came opposite the wooden seat. He paused and looked at Tumulty. There was a pink celluloid covering over his left eye and a piece of black tape, attached to the celluloid, passed around his forehead and his skull. He scratched his shoulders against his clothes, grinned, showing three teeth, and then again he raised his stick, saluting. He took a pace forward and then saluted McDara, also with his upraised stick. He shuffled on, grinning, halted in front of Fetch and again he raised his stick, for the third time, saluting. Then he passed on. Their eyes were fixed on the white back of his smock. He passed on, shuffling, poking at refuse, until he rounded the bend.

The three men sighed. McDara looked at his watch. Fetch and Tumulty started when McDara looked at his watch. They eyed the watch. Then they eyed his eyes when he had looked at the watch. He put the watch back into his pocket and nodded his head. They each made jerky movements with

their heads and with their right arms. Fetch's eyes
again looked down the road.

Then, suddenly, his hand, holding the cigarette,
was thrust farther out, over the front door of the car,
towards them. His body became rigid. Their bodies
became rigid. His face began to convulse. His eyes
narrowed. His forehead wrinkled. His eyebrows
contracted. He lowered his head, peering closely.
Then his lower lip expanded and thrust upwards.
He raised his hand slowly, held it aloft for two
seconds and then dropped the cigarette to the road.
He pulled in his hand and settled his bowler hat
forward on his head, crushing it down far on to his
skull.

McDara and Tumulty dropped their cigarettes on
to the road. McDara stamped on the butt of his
cigarette. He signed to Tumulty. Tumulty was gazing fiercely at Fetch, with distended eyes. McDara
growled and stamped on Tumulty's cigarette end,
scraping his foot several times on the road where
it had fallen. Tumulty rose to his feet. McDara
caught him by the sleeve and pulled him down.
Tumulty opened his lips and looked aghast at Mc-
Dara. McDara's face was now deadly pale, but his
eyes glowed and his lips were puckered up. Then
he pointed his finger at Fetch and set his teeth.
Tumulty's head shot round on his thick neck. His
eyes remained fixed on Fetch's hat.

Fetch was now crouching forward in the driver's
seat of the car. His head was twisted around to the

right. It moved hither and thither and his eyes blinked rapidly. He was watching a man, who approached up the road, that led southwards from the wooden seat.

Fetch raised his hat. McDara and Tumulty got to their feet slowly. With a sudden movement of his right hand, Fetch pulled out his pistol and thrust it down between his knees. He cocked it with his left hand and then remained motionless.

The man was coming near. He was a tall man. He wore a brown hat, with the rim slightly lowered in front, over his forehead. He wore blue trousers, carefully creased. He wore a dark brown overcoat that was narrow at the waist. He wore white spats and black shoes. There was a silver pin in his tie. He walked erect, with his eyes on the ground. He had razor lips and a long nose. His eyes were cruel. His complexion was sallow. He walked with great determination, rapidly. One hand was in his pocket. The other hand, covered with a glove that looked white in the distance, carried a walking-stick. The walking-stick had a silver knob. His small feet struck the pavement daintily, making a little movement, when raised, as if they were kicking something trivial out of their path.

He smiled once, as he approached. When he smiled, he raised his head, glanced furtively to the right, over the orchard wall, and then his face grew dark and serious as his eyes returned to the ground.

Fetch turned on the engine and started the car.

The engine began to purr. McDara and Tumulty, stepping lightly, moved slowly to the corner of the road, up which the man was walking towards them. A tree, overhanging the wall, cast a shadow on them with its branches. The shadow covered Tumulty's head and shoulders. A little twig drew an imaginary dark scar across McDara's forehead with its shadow.

The man's steps were now audible. Tumulty's face grew white and then flushed dark-red. McDara raised his right foot and tapped his left ankle three times.

Suddenly a large, yellow car came rapidly from the west. The man was now within ten yards of the corner. Fetch got out of his car on the far side. Tumulty drew his revolver from his pocket. The driver of the yellow car raised his head. His eyes and his mouth opened wide. He looked around him wildly and then stamped on the accelerator. The yellow car dashed past at a great speed. McDara drew his revolver. Fetch appeared at the head of the motor-car, with his right hand behind his back.

The man reached the corner of the road, walking with his eyes on the ground.

'Now,' said McDara.

The man stopped dead and raised his eyes, holding his walking-stick horizontally in front of him.

'Give it to the bastard,' said Fetch, taking a pace forward with his left leg and raising his pistol.

Tumulty plunged forward and fired. The man's face contorted as if with grotesque laughter. He jumped about an inch off the ground, swayed backwards slightly and then hurtled forward, with his hand on his chest. He dropped his walking-stick. McDara fired and the man turned slightly to the right. Then Fetch bared his teeth and fired. The man paused in the middle of the road, shook his head and raised his hands. There was a dark spot on his face. They rushed towards him. All three of them fired simultaneously. He made a gurgling sound and fell forward on his face. He raised his hips. Another bullet struck him in the back. He turned round on his side.

Fetch, growling like an animal, put his foot on the writhing body and laid it flat, with its face to the sun. Then he pressed down the stomach with his foot and began to fire, saying with each shot: 'Huh.'

McDara stood still, with his mouth open and his smoking revolver held out in front of him, staring at the sky.

Tumulty stood behind Fetch, holding out his revolver and muttering:

'Here. Take this. Give him more.'

'He's all right now,' said Fetch. 'Come on, boys.'

They ran towards the car.

The fallen man's stomach heaved slightly. His lower lip kept striking his upper lip, like the ticking of a little watch. A big pool of dark-red blood oozed out about his shattered head.

The three men entered the car. The car rushed

forward. Tumulty fired two shots into the air. The car dashed around the corner at full speed, past an old woman, who stood there, transfixed. The old woman, with her hands held up, half shielding her eyes, gazed at the fallen man. Then she uttered a wild shriek and began to turn round and round on the road.

A man in shirt-sleeves, with his coat, held in his right hand, trailing after him, dashed up the road past the old woman and reached the fallen man. He knelt by the body and listened, with his ear to the heaving stomach. Then he rose and dashed on, shouting out at the top of his voice:

'Murder! Murder! Help!'

People came from all directions. They ran to the body. A little man with a beard knelt by the body, raised his arms up to the sky and began to recite the Act of Contrition. Another man caught up the body in his arms, staggered under his load and began to repeat foolishly:

'Where am I goin' to take him to?'

A huge fellow with a gruff voice came up and said:

'Put him on this coat. Prop up his head.'

There was a crowd. Their faces were frenzied. Loud cries, curses, prayers and lamentations rose in a confused medley.

Then a little man with a yellow face, wearing large spectacles, crawled in through the crowd on his hands and knees, until he got to the pool of dark-red blood. He dipped his hand in it. It had curdled and the blood-froth reached to his wrist. The little fellow stood up and raised his frenzied face to the sky.

'Make way, make way,' he cried to the people. 'Make way for the Sign of the Lord.'

They stepped back and he walked through them, with his knees trembling, to the corner of the grey orchard wall. He reached the wall. Then, with a grotesque gesture, he struck his chest, twisted his body, held out his gory hand and made the Sign of the Cross with the blood, on the wall. Then he pointed to the crooked bloody cross he had made and burst into a peal of hysterical laughter.

A dog began to bark within the orchard and a flock of birds, terrified by the barking, flew up into the blue sky, twittering.

CHAPTER NINETEEN

THE city clocks were striking twelve. McDara entered a big church that was crowded with people. He dipped his hand in the holy-water font and crossed himself, touching his brow, his breast and his shoulders. Then, holding his shabby cap in his left hand, he moved towards a pillar and genuflected near it, saluting the high altar, up which the priest was ascending, bearing the covered chalice in front of his throat with both hands.

McDara rose from his knee and stood in the shadow of the dusty pillar with his eyes on the altar. With a loud murmur of feet, the huge congregation knelt on both knees and bowed their heads. Mc-Dara also knelt.

He was now dressed in his old shabby raincoat and his wrinkled blue trousers, as he had been that day he arrived at Mrs. Buggy's house in Hardwicke Street. He had the same stoop in his shoulders, the same frown on his pallid face, the same pale, nervous hands. But his eyes were different.

They were now fixed in a stupid stare, without any movement of the eyeballs. They glanced slowly around the gloomy church, that seemed to be all enveloped in a thick coat of dust. They glanced at the glittering altar, with its plaster saints, its rich cloths and its gaudy ornaments. They glanced at the windows, through which the sunlight streamed in many weird colours through the stained glass. But they avoided the people that knelt all round, breathing loudly and emitting a smell of humanity.

His eyes had become visionless. They saw but they did not record what they saw. For his mind was not receiving their impressions. It was fixed on the spot where HE had fallen, with a dark mark on his face and his right eye showing only the white of the eyeball.

The priest turned round on the altar. He walked down the steps to the base. He stood on the strip of carpet with his feet close together. He began the Mass.

'*Introibo ad altare dei*,' he cried out in a lazy, bored voice.

McDara started. The stupid stare slowly vanished from his eyes. His face softened. His lips moved. Then his eyes gleamed merrily and his body shook with silent laughter. Looking steadily at the priest's back, upon which the vestment gleamed, he bared his teeth in a grin and whispered to himself:

'That's a lie. The lout cannot approach the altar of God. There is no God.'

With head upraised over the bowed heads of the congregation, he stared boldly at the priest's back and at the glittering altar. His face looked beautiful with exaltation. He grew joyous, feeling a strange accession of youth and freshness, as something heavy passed from his mind, lightening his body. He grew excited with this casting out of something that had lain heavy on him; just as a tawny snake, casting off its sun-tanned hide, revels in ecstasy as the skin falls from its sinuous body and then, feeling fresh and lissom in its new-born coat, with the joy of voluptuous youth it swims on its slippery belly through the tangled grass.

He was experiencing the exaltation of the animal that has just buried its fangs in its prey. His mind, exhausted by the long preparation, the torture of anxiety and the actual physical effort of the act itself, had remained fixed in a stupor until the priest spoke the first words of the Mass. Now it began to exult, to boast of what it had done. And the furious pleasure he derived from this boasting momentarily raised him to a lofty peak, from which he could look down in spirit, on the whole universe. There it lay, a trivial, simple thing, easy to understand.

This state of sublime ecstasy did not last long, but in such a state time is of no consequence. He experienced such a happiness while it lasted and his mind created such fantasies of power and limitless understanding, that his personality seemed to him to expand like a balloon, crushing before its bulging walls, gods, laws, societies and planets. He transcended his human shape in his imagination. Almost in the same moment, he saw himself, like Samson, catching the pillars of the church and crushing them into dust, flying to Saturn and laying it waste and explaining to an enormous multitude a new scientific discovery that would abolish death.

Then he passed out of that state, just as strangely

as he had entered it. A sleepiness overcame him. His visions became less and less ecstatic. His head began to sink. His neck seemed powerless to hold it up. His limbs became heavy, as with sickness. Fear flowed into his brain, in the form of a mist, and he bobbed his head slowly up and down, in mute acknowledgment of its existence.

And he said to himself, forming the words with his lips but making no sound:

'Mother, I always loved you.'

And in answer to this unuttered sentence, his mother's figure appeared to him, imaged in the air, somewhere beyond his left shoulder. He could see distinctly the skin on her fat wrists. The skin on her fat wrists had always shone, as if polished. He could also see her lips. There was a slight down on her upper lip and a little mole at the right corner. He also felt her eyes. He could not make her eyes look at him and he dared not look towards them. But he knew they shone with love. And this love, his mother's love, pained him exceedingly. The pain of a love that cannot be satisfied, that is for ever lost, filled the whole interior of his body and clogged his throat and it became so violent that he thought his heart would burst.

He saw himself as a little child, with his hands raised up to the sky, howling for his mother, standing in a green field, after sunset, with the air getting cold and the cries of the birds becoming strange whispers. What horror! Although he could feel her

near, she never answered his call for help, and
although the impression of her soft arms was as real
to him as the moisture of his tongue, he could not
reach her arms. His head kept reaching forward,
trying to reach the pure warmth of her bosom, and
his ears kept listening for the soft crooning sound
that came from her lips, when she fondled his naked
toes. But the more he longed, the more some extraordinary and devilish force dragged him back, making an enormous chasm between him and her.

And then wrinkling his forehead, he bared his
teeth and whispered to himself, in abject despair:

'She is dead. She cannot hear me.'

And then he raised his eyes humbly towards the
glittering altar and muttered:

'Oh! Christ! What loneliness!'

For a moment the pale face of the crucified Christ
became real in his imagination. And he loved the
face. The pillared, high-domed, dusty church also
became real and friendly, the abode of Christly love,
and his eyes swelled with tears, as he suddenly
abandoned himself to a feeling of submission. Like
a rushing wave, this feeling came upon him. He
bowed his head slowly and he made himself one with
the bowed, kneeling people, asking forgiveness from
the pale face of the crucified Christ. But scarcely had
he willed this submission, when he saw mocking
faces instead of the pale face of Christ. His lips
drew back. His lowered head became taut and it
jerked upwards. The tears had dried in his eyes and

221

a terrible ferocity took the place of the feeling of submission.

He looked around him cunningly, saw the bowed
heads of the people, and saw them sombrely, as
dreaded enemies. He saw them as beings alien to
his own nature, with the same feeling of repulsion
that a man, when close to a beast, suddenly sees in his
mind a furtive, fleeting picture and is carried back
through countless centuries to some remote unrecog-
nizable place and then, without thinking, looks at
the beast's hide and his nostrils become full of a rank
odour and his blood grows warm with a primitive
instinct and his eyes glance to one side, as if in fear,
and he feels a strange shame, as in the presence
of a relative who has become abject and loathsome
through crime, debauchery and decadence.

The people rose to their feet as the priest crossed
the altar. He rose with them. Then his mind func-
tioned clearly and actively and yet it did not function
directly, as a normal mind, but slightly projected into
a dream state. For it still transformed the impressions of his senses into composite pictures and he
felt the people about him, not as individuals but as
a herd, composed of things alien to his nature, as
wild horses, buffaloes, bees resting on a bush. The
priest, the altar-boys, the images of saints in plaster,
the sunrays painted by the stained glass, all assumed
a different significance. And it hurt him to find
them on this lower plane, for henceforth he realized
that he must stand or move alone on a higher plane,

and he saw how horrible it would be, should a man, followed by a dog, suddenly turn around and imagine himself to be a dog and begin to bark and run around after his imaginary tail, which he had lost by becoming a man, through some giant and painful effort in the forgotten past.

He felt that he was perspiring and he put up his hand to his forehead to brush away the moisture. But instead of finding his forehead moist, he found it dry as parchment and very hot. He drew in a deep breath through his teeth with a hissing sound. A cloud seemed to draw back from his mind and, as when a curtain is drawn from a bedroom window on a lovely summer morning, showing to the awakened senses of the risen sleeper a meadow gleaming with sunlit dew, a stream flowing between willows and a distant mountain, cinctured with low clouds and a summit upon which the mica gleams, like jewels in the crown of a king, so he felt the joy of living. And he thought with abounding pleasure of the delight of running barefoot over short, smooth grass.

'I am alive,' he said to himself. 'I am alive. *Laudate dominum omnes gentes.* I am alive.'

The people knelt again. He knelt. Now a weight seemed to press upon him from above, thrusting him downwards into a thick-walled cavern, and he heard the clanking of chains and the distant murmurs of men, invisible, talking near by in sombre voices, and the dull thud of gruesome feet. The cavern was in darkness and time passed there like a sombre

223

cloud, making a sound, like the sound of summer on a sultry noon, when life drowses and the grass sways with the wallowing of hidden insects and nothing moves but the jaws and the wagging ears of prostrate sheep. Then, blinded, by the darkness of the cavern, he felt himself dragged out into a cold dawn, to a scaffold, which he ascended trembling. With terrible distinctness he felt his neck enter the ice-cold noose.

Then he distended his eyes, bit his protruding tongue and looked about him. The people were prostrate, the bell was ringing on the altar, the priest was holding aloft the body and blood of Christ. He lowered his head and struck his breast with great violence. And while he was striking his breast, he understood why he could not get his mother's eyes to turn towards him. He had lost the innocence of his childhood. He had lost the God of his childhood and also the people of his childhood. And if he went back among them, rending his garments, like the ancient Jews, they would look at him strangely and then turn away their eyes, just as his mother did.

The people raised their heads. He raised his head and muttered to himself calmly:

'Very well, then.'

Now the whole earth became dry and parched. His mind was barren, incapable of thought. And eternity was such, barren, without motion, a summer noonday, with insects wallowing in the grass and all mankind motionless, waiting for nothing, for nothing would ever happen.

The people rose and knelt. The dreary, bored voice of the priest floated through the dusty church, with terrible languor, as if the human voice were long since weary of declaiming those words, about the Christ that had been crucified to the cries of joy of the same human voice. In terrible weariness, McDara listened to the dreary words, lisped, muttered and let fall like daubs of clotted blood on to the bowed heads of the people, and he knew that he was a murderer.

'A murderer!'

The two words, one small and slight, without meaning, the other large and heavy, like a ball of lead, resounded in his brain. For an instant, he waited with horror, expecting his mind to become full of horrible visions and accusations. But nothing happened. The two words departed and his mind remained empty and barren, as silent as death.

And in that state, perfectly silent and barren, he waited, breathing painfully, until the Mass ended and the people rose to leave the church.

He rose with them and walked out, with stooping shoulders, dazed, thoughtless.

CHAPTER TWENTY

'MURDERER!'

That extraordinary word again reverberated somewhere near him as he stepped forth into the open air
from the porch of the dusty church. The sunlight
glittered. There was a cold purity in the windless
air which strangely reminded him of his childhood;
emerging thus on Sunday, after Mass, from the
parish church, on a spring day, the air had been
coldly pure and the sunlight had glittered; the world
had been full of a miraculous wisdom and innocence,
manifesting itself in pure smells, brilliant lights
and merry sounds. How the sunbeams had danced
on the old, yellow, wooden gate of the church-
yard!

Here (Oh! God!) they danced just the same,
but on bleak house walls that were hoary with dirt
and sin. And all round there was no sound of innocence, no gentle sheep feeding in a green field,
no rivulet whispering a song of joy; nothing but
sordidness and confinement.

Here that horrifying word rang out, unuttered but
very loud, reverberating through the narrow channels
of the streets, rebounding on the dusty pavements,
screeching up alleyways, grinning on the signboards
of shops, written in red letters on the foreheads of
terrified people.

They had heard the news. Newsboys were on the
streets. People were snatching at the papers. Ex-

cited cries issued from lips that had just read the words printed on the black, blurred columns.

'God have mercy on us.'

'The earth should open up and swallow them.'

'Shot down like a dog in his prime.'

'The only hope of the country gone.'

'Now what's going to happen to us?'

Standing on the pavement's edge, in front of a closed public-house, he heard these cries, with a fixed expression on his face. And that other imaginary cry of MURDERER kept ringing loudly in his brain. He felt utterly helpless, for it was now suddenly revealed to him that, although his mind had been carried aloft by the commission of this act on to an inhuman plane, where all emotions were non-existent, his body still remained capable of suffering. He knew that it was a weak, trifling body, a mean thing, that had conceived and executed an enormity through vanity, cowardice and jealousy. His mind pitied it and, pitying it, suffered with it, far more than it could suffer, if they had been equal, his mind and body. For out of this act, both in the contemplation and the execution of it, an extraordinary understanding had come, of good and evil.

'They won't get far,' said an angry voice beside him.

'But what's the use?' said another voice in despair. 'The damage is done. Look at the horrible mark this'll leave on the soul of the people. Assassins in cold blood.'

These words hurt McDara's flesh, just as if each word had been a needle, thrust into his body. He moved away from them down the street, walking very stiffly, making a shuddering sound with his tongue against the roof of his mouth. He came to a narrow lane where a crowd of poor people had gathered. The lane looked dark. He decided to turn up that way, for it seemed better to be in a dark, narrow place, than in a wide street.

Passing through the group at the mouth of the lane, he heard them also talking of it. But they talked in a different way, and he halted, eagerly listening, hoping to hear some voice forgive him. But they talked of it with interest, as of a spectacle that had been provided for their amusement.

'They turned a machine-gun on him from an armoured car,' said one.

'He had a breast-plate under his waistcoat,' said another. 'They were pumpin' lead into him for a quarter of an hour before they knocked him down.'

'Them fellahs are in the mountains be now,' said another. 'Ye'll see some queer rallies before the night is out.'

'Be Janey,' said another, with a laugh, 'the best place is under the bed from now on.'

McDara leaned against the window of a little barber's shop. He felt overcome with weakness. His body had become limp. But his mind became enraged. He had to raise his head and open his mouth, both to relieve the weakness of his bowels by drawing in a large draught of air and also to let out the cry of agony that swelled up in his mind.

'God! God! Nobody will ever understand why I did it.'

His mouth closed and he lowered his head. The weakness passed and he became nervous. Had he been acting suspiciously? He looked about him with cunning, now in terror for his safety. He saw a man looking at him. He glared fiercely at the man. The man smiled faintly and lowered his eyes to a packet of cigarettes which McDara had taken out of his pocket and which he held in his hand without opening. McDara looked at the packet and then suddenly, without knowing why, held it towards the stranger. The stranger raised his eyelids and his face became suffused with a joyous light. A lump came into McDara's throat. He wanted to throw himself on the stranger's chest and burst into tears. The stranger opened the packet of cigarettes eagerly, took one and handed the packet back to McDara. McDara smiled and he felt happier at that moment than he had ever felt in his life. The stranger, holding the cigarette in his hand, began to make foolish movements with his body, like a person who has just received a very precious gift. McDara handed him a box of matches. He muttered something and lit his cigarette. McDara drew in a deep breath and began to light a cigarette himself. Then they both leaned against the window of the barber's shop. Neither spoke. Both were, to all appearances, listening to the excited conversation of the crowd.

The stranger was a very tall, lean man. He was remarkably like McDara, except that he was much taller and the expression of his face was very mild. He had a weak mouth. The similarity arose from the sense of mystery and of suffering suggested by both their faces; their pallor, their deep eyes, their habit of gazing vacantly into the distance. But whereas McDara's eyes, gazing into the distance, inspired a feeling of terror, the stranger's eyes only inspired pity. His clothes were very shabby and yet spotlessly clean. His fingers were very long and the nails on the third fingers were nibbled to the quick. His ears rested flatly against his skull. They also were very long and their tips shone. He was wearing a cap and a suit of blue serge that had several patches on it. And yet, he had a very dignified appearance. Even the way he held his cigarette, between his thumb and the first two fingers, was dignified.

A military motor lorry, loaded with soldiers, who carried their weapons in readiness for use, came down the street. It came at a fast pace, tooting loudly. There was silence as it passed and then everybody followed it.

'Now ye'll see the hue an' cry,' said a little fellow, as he ran after the lorry.

McDara and the stranger were left alone, leaning against the barber's window.

'Something very exciting must have happened,' said the stranger to McDara in a listless voice.

McDara looked at him with surprise. Then he became suspicious.

'How do you mean?' he said.

The stranger flushed and trembled slightly. McDara's sharp voice terrified him. He waved his cigarette in the direction in which the lorry had gone.

'There's a raid,' he said. 'Something must have happened. I heard a stop press a minute ago. It appears somebody has been shot dead.'

Then he looked at McDara timorously, with a vacant stare in his gentle eyes. McDara looked at the man closely. Then he understood. The man was starving. He was almost an idiot through hunger. That dazed, vacant stare became suddenly familiar and he remembered his childhood; at the beginning of spring, when the harvest had been consumed through the long winter, men used to look like that, with a queer dazed look in their eyes. They used to fall down in the road. His mother also had fallen one day and there was green moisture on her lips, as if she had been eating weeds.

He turned excitedly to the stranger and said furiously:

'Yes, a man has been shot dead. Maybe some starving man went mad with hunger and shot him. Why should people be hungry in this country?

When I was a little boy my mother nearly died of hunger. There are still people dying of hunger. And while there is hunger people will go mad and kill one another. Eh?'

The stranger started and glanced about him furtively, with fear.

'No starving man did it,' he whispered. 'A starving man can't kill anybody.'

'Eh?' said McDara fiercely. He began to tremble. 'And so you think it's possible for other people to be happy and sane while men are starving? I don't think so. In fact, I'm certain of it.'

The stranger drew himself up wearily against the window and made an attempt to look sternly at McDara. His countenance trembled and little glimmers of light shone irregularly through his eyes, as if he were trying to get into an angry mood. But he failed to do so. His body became slack again and he said in a timid voice:

'Perhaps you would not make these references if you knew that I am practically starving at this moment. And that . . . that it's through my own fault. I'm not morally justified . . . I mean there's no moral justification, as far as I'm concerned, for . . . for unconsidered action.'

The stranger's lips trembled as he spoke. He uttered the words in an artificial tone, like a speech delivered by an envoy to a foreign gathering, and he was obviously thinking quite different words but was afraid to utter them.

McDara's eyes blazed, and for some reason he wanted to throttle the stranger.

'So you are hungry,' he said fiercely.

The stranger put his thin hands into his shabby sleeves and looked sideways at McDara. He did not reply.

'Well, then,' said McDara, 'come and eat with me. I'm like you. Why shouldn't we eat together? I know you're like me. You see, I too am down an' out. Eh? You can see that, can't you?'

A sudden change came over the stranger. As it were, he stepped eagerly and without shame, naked, from behind the little wall of pride which had been shielding him. And he exposed the bestial expression born of hunger in his countenance. With a servile smile, he took McDara's arm and began to mutter words of thanks, prayers and blessings. Shrugging his shoulders, he began to point his finger down the lane, saying that there was a good place down there, that he had not eaten for two days, that he had stood all night with another fellow, against the wall of a house, where there was a big furnace, that the nuns had fed him all last week, but that he was ashamed to go any more to them. He couldn't stand the look in their eyes. He had been thinking all morning how pleasant it would be to die, but that it was impossible to die, or to have the courage to kill oneself in a starving condition. And he also said in a queer whisper that what he had been saying just now was untrue, because, before McDara had come up, he had been thinking of the assassination with considerable joy and wishing that it was he himself who had done it.

'But never in all my life,' he said, with great emphasis, 'have I been able to come to any decision. On any question. Never. They give good food here and it's cheap. It may not be exceptionally clean, but it's good and the people are kind.'

McDara walked along beside the man, with a savage frown on his face. He felt that the stranger was dragging him downwards, out of the world he knew, into another world, inhabited by helpless beings, and that he would never again manage to get back into the world of his childhood. He felt that he was a doomed man and that this stranger, with the shining ears, who was simpering beside him, was some sort of curious devil, whose business it was to convey doomed people into hell.

And yet, with another part of himself, a humble, contrite part, he was weeping imaginary tears and feeling that it was good to be merciful and kind and that happiness was just such a feeling, the salty taste of a mother's happy tears on the lips of a child who had strayed and had been found again.

And at the same time, making a sound like water boiling in a pot, that other word MURDERER still kept reverberating at a distance. It had now become a large uncouth ball and it was being tossed about in the air by a great concourse of savage, red-eyed people. Were it not for its existence and the savagery of the people, he felt that life could be a glorious thing and that he could halt this stranger in the laneway, raise his hand to the sky and tell him wonderful things, about rivulets and sheep on a spring day and an old yellow, wooden gate, upon which the sunrays were dancing.

They became silent, walking along side by side. The stranger was so weak with hunger, that he staggered as he walked and his body stumbled against McDara's. Every time he stumbled, he started and said: 'I'm very sorry.' They walked through several lanes and dirty streets. Then they went down a steep hill into a wide street, where there were very old houses. At last they halted in front of a house that had a sign hanging over its door. There was nothing painted on the sign and God only knows why it had been hung up there. Probably somebody hung it up there and then forgot to have it painted. In the window, on a long dish, there was a ham, looking mouldy, with sprigs of parsley around it. They entered the house, going down two steps to a stone floor. An enormous open hearth faced the door. There was a remarkably high grate, full of blazing coal. From an outstanding iron hook, there hung a short chain over the fire and to the chain was attached a huge pot. On the hob there was a black kettle almost as large as the pot. The tables in this strange eating-room were concealed between wooden partitions, that ran down the length of the room on one side. On the other side, between the window and the fire, the landlady sat at a table upon which there was a white cloth, a money till, knives, forks, plates and a petticoat that was being sewed. The kitchen opened off the back of the room. In there, two people, a man and a woman, could be seen rushing about, preparing food. The place looked ancient. A brass plate, like a shield, hanging over the fire, made it look still more ancient and mysterious.

They passed several enclosures until they came to the far table by the kitchen door. That table was unoccupied. They pushed their way in to the far end, one on either side of the table. The landlady, a great old woman, with flaming eyes, shouted out in a hoarse voice:

'Beef or mutton?'

The stranger whispered to McDara that he preferred mutton.

'Mutton,' said McDara.

'Mutton for two,' said the landlady, polishing a fork with a napkin.

Almost immediately, a man, wearing a dirty apron, rushed out of the kitchen, leaned over their table and began to hurl knives, forks, spoons and little plates towards them. At the same time, with a rag which he held in his other hand, he wiped the table with a great gesture, casting the refuse belonging to previous meals on to the sawdust-covered floor.

McDara sat with furrowed forehead and his hands

clasped between his knees. The stranger kept biting the third fingers of his hands, one after the other. Suddenly he whispered across the table:

'My name is Lawless. What's yours?'

McDara looked up at him slowly, narrowed his eyes and said in a low whisper:

'My name is Carter.'

'No offence,' said Lawless timidly. 'I didn't mean to be curious, only just that you've been . . . I just wanted . . .'

McDara coughed and looked at Lawless fiercely. A thought came into his mind that it would be a good thing to take his belt off, give the money to Lawless and hand himself over to the police. Then perhaps that word MURDERER would not be reverberating all the time at a distance. At the same time, he felt himself becoming possessed by a furious hatred of this fellow with the shining ears.

The waiter, moving with the same savage rapidity, served their meals. He almost hurled the plates at them, muttering as he did so:

'Three an' eight.'

McDara took out some money and paid him. Lawless, as soon as the food was put in front of him, began to eat, not rapidly but slowly, with trembling hands. McDara also began to eat. They finished the meal without speaking.

'I must get rid of this fellow now and go,' thought McDara. 'I must go and find the others. Eh? How am I going to look them in the eyes? That part of me is dead. If only I could get back into that mood and keep on hating. Now my hatred is scattered. Every trivial thing is an enemy. And I am a house-less dog, begging at the door of humanity.'

'I say?' said Lawless.

McDara looked at him. The man's face had un-accountably changed. It now looked morose and selfish. There was a sneaking look in the mild eyes.

'Could I have your address?' he said. 'Some day perhaps I might be able to get on my feet again and repay you . . . for this meal.'

'I have no address,' said McDara sombrely. 'I told you I am like yourself. I'm going to Liverpool to-night. I'm a sailor.'

'Even so,' said Lawless. 'I might . . .'

Then he started and bit his finger.

'I wish I were a sailor,' he said.

McDara narrowed his eyes and thought:

'Why am I wasting time here with this fellow? I should be up and about.'

'You know,' said Lawless, 'I have drifted about all my life and I never seem to do anything. Even now, the thought of going to sea terrifies me. I wonder why that is.'

McDara did not reply.

'Yes,' continued Lawless. 'Life is very queer. You know, it always puzzles me why we are afraid to die. Yet I'm afraid to die as much as any man,

238

even a man with a wife and family and property, a successful citizen.'

'What were you?' said McDara harshly. 'A schoolmaster?'

'No,' said Lawless listlessly. 'I was never really anything. Would you care to hear my story?'

'Better give him a few shillings and get rid of him,' thought McDara. 'Even now, Tumulty and Fetch may be concocting some stunt that'll prevent my getting away.'

Then he thought:

'It would be dangerous to go there yet. I may as well stay here.'

'Go ahead,' he said aloud.

The tramp, whom McDara had seen in the betting shop, now came into the room, bringing a heavy smell with him. There were drops of moisture on his beard, as if he had just been drinking. His eyes were blood-shot. He was still wearing two overcoats. He stood in the middle of the floor and looked about him fiercely, as if challenging all in the room. He was a powerful and menacing fellow. He hailed the landlady in a loud voice and then went to the fire. He held his hands over the blaze.

'Three runnin' doubles I got,' he said. 'An' the divil a drop I tasted till Saturday at one o'clock. Now I haven't the price of a meal. There's no luck in horses.'

He addressed the room, but nobody replied. Then he laughed aloud and began to clap his hands together. He struck the hearthstone with his heel and said in a fierce voice:

'Well! Anyway, to hell with Dublin. The sun is shinin', boys, and there's a woman in Dundalk that keeps a lodgin'-house. Before the larks are up to-morrow morning I'll be after lyin' in her bed. Here's for the man with the hair on his chest.'

He laughed again, struck his chest a violent blow and left the room. As he disappeared out the door, shaking his moist beard, a voice within McDara's brain said:

'Get up and follow him.'

He got to his feet, but Lawless hurriedly caught him by the sleeve and pulled him down.

'Don't go yet,' said Lawless nervously. 'It's so seldom I meet anybody to talk to. I don't want to sponge on you, but I am terribly alone and perhaps I'll never again pass in by the door I came out; never again meet anybody but brutes without mind.'

'Well!' said McDara. 'What is the use of talking to me, then? I am a brute without mind.'

Suddenly he smiled at Lawless, overcome by a malicious whimsy.

'I'll terrify this lout,' he thought.

'No, no,' said Lawless. 'You are a good man, although you may not think you are. There is nothing that a man is more afraid of than being good. I can see in your eyes that you are good. Forgive me speaking like this, but I am over forty now and I have been drifting for ten years. If I had a genius for expressing my knowledge of life, there are many things I could add to the store of human wisdom.'

'Why not?' thought McDara. 'If I am an outcast and that word is going to resound for ever in my ears, let me be a complete and pitiless devil. After all, there is in that a possibility of great power. Hatred and callousness are more potent than the whimpering sentimentality of that fellow. See what it has brought him to?'

'I, on the other hand, am a bad man,' said Lawless, 'and I drifted downwards because I discovered it and tried to be good. It's the bad natures, and I mean weak by bad, that are overcome by despair when they see the corruption of life. I'd give anything to be strong for one year and do something great. That would make me believe in myself. Even something that would make people afraid of me. You know the greatest torture is to be despised by everybody. I have often gone to prison gates and accused myself of crimes, but they wouldn't take me in.'

'And you have never done anything wrong in your life?' said McDara, suddenly interested. 'You have never committed any crime?'

'Never,' said Lawless, hiding his hands in his sleeves, as if ashamed of their impotence.

'Yet you're not happy?'

'No.'

'You don't feel innocent? You don't feel in contact with your childhood, if you understand what I mean?'

241

'There is no such thing as innocence,' said Lawless listlessly. 'You know I was once a prominent public man in this city. I was going to tell you the story of my life. Would you care to hear it?'

'Well, then,' said McDara. 'Supposing I were to give you three hundred and sixty-five pounds now, would that make you happy?'

The stranger looked at him for a moment with cunning and then his expression changed to one of horror.

'Now I don't like you,' he said brutally. 'A moment ago, you were a friend sitting there. Now you're a . . .'

McDara leaned across the table and said with his eyes glittering:

'Go on. Say the word. If you say that word I'll give you . . .'

He smiled and the stranger's face trembled.

'Five shillings,' said McDara, laughing. 'Here you are. Take it. I have learned something from you. Do you know that? You've given me an idea. Would you believe that?'

He put two half-crowns on the table in front of the stranger. The stranger looked at them without touching them. Then he looked up at McDara. The look of horror was still in his eyes.

'I'm very sorry for you,' he said.

McDara's mood changed. He made a great effort, trying to retain something that was slipping from him. Then he laughed again.

'You didn't say the word, but you can keep the money. Maybe if you had said the word it would no longer be necessary for you to be sorry for anything. However . . . Good-bye. Good luck.'

He got up and left the room hurriedly.

CHAPTER TWENTY-ONE

It was now after two o'clock. The city was in a tumult. The streets were crowded. There was hardly any noise. But the subdued excitement was more menacing than the loudest noise. Every face was sombre. Everywhere, agents of the Government moved about, halting motor-cars, searching pedestrians for arms. All the bridges were blocked by pickets of police and detectives. Soldiers in lorries and armoured cars dashed along at a furious pace, with weapons in their hands. And yet all the excitement and bustle seemed to have no purpose. The movements of the people suggested the stupefied agitation of a nest of insects, whose structure has suddenly been overthrown by the unwitting step of some large animal and they are dashing about, with objects in their tiny mouths or held between their legs, searching and scurrying to and fro, seeking the intruder, although it is quite beyond their power to find the intruder or to punish him or indeed to remedy the mischief he has caused.

Their eyes and their wits sought feverishly for the hidden force that had struck at them, while the intruder walked among them, clad in a shabby, whitish raincoat, with pallid cheeks and stooping shoulders, with a forlorn look in his jaded eyes. They eyed him as he passed, with indifference, for he looked no monster. He did not look big or menacing. His thin, blue-veined hands did not seem capable of wielding an enormous weapon. There was no lust of power in his sunken eyes. His slack, lifting footsteps were not hurried like those of a fugitive criminal; or of a warrior, who dashes on winged feet into the tribal camp, slays the chieftain with his gleaming sword and then flies into the forest, scattering fallen twigs and bursting through dry brushwood, while the unloosed hounds bay in his track.

Nobody challenged McDara. Neither was he afraid that anybody might challenge him. In this strange world, into which he had passed after the act, the fear of the flesh was non-existent. But its nonexistence inspired him with a greater fear than fear itself. Just as informers present themselves before the rulers of their organizations and demand that they be killed before they kill themselves, seeking escape from the cries of their wounded consciences in death, so he was inspired with an inhuman terror by the helplessness of the beings he saw about him, pursuing him and yet allowing him to pass unheeded. Just as if he wore an invisible cloak. But he was unable to experience the mania of confession which inspires the informer, that desire for contact with the lost herd, even through the medium of death at the hands of the herd. His state of inhumanity had assumed complete possession of him, so that all men had become so alien, that it was just as impossible for him to feel their emotions or to establish contact with their reason as it might be to establish reasonable contact with the mind of an infant.

Protected by this awful remoteness from any expression of nervousness, he descended into the city, passed through Dame Street and College Green and then turned northwards towards the river. It was only when he was crossing the river by O'Connell Bridge that a momentary feeling of despair took possession of him. He wanted to hurl his body over the bridge into the river. But he passed on without heeding this desire. And when he passed the bridge, he again felt cool outwardly, contemplating the vacuum into which his heated mind had transformed the universe.

In this state of stupor, he was completely unaware of the purpose of his movements and he had passed northwards by the Nelson Pillar, when the face of a young man standing near the doorway of a shop made him start and recover consciousness. He only saw the young man's face for three or four seconds, but he noted every peculiarity of the countenance, the bony jaws, the high cheekbones, the long nose, the half-open, soft lips and the eyes. The eyes were fixed in an extraordinary stare. They glittered. McDara recognized that glitter, although he was not aware of ever having seen it before. But he had felt it in his own eyes. It was the glitter that comes into the eyes when a mind begins to enjoy the ecstasy of contemplated assassination. The young man, standing there on the pavement, was enacting the assassination in his mind and finding pleasure in it.

And McDara thought:

'Have I reproduced myself? Am I no longer alone?'

That was equally terrifying; even more so. He had passed the young man and gone about fifty yards when this thought expressed itself in his mind. He immediately turned about and, walking quickly, came up to the spot where the young man stood, with the intention of speaking to him and saying:

'It has no meaning.'

But instead of speaking to the young man, he looked at him contemptuously and passed on. He turned to the right, down Mary Street, now aware that he was going to Tumulty's room, 'to put the tin hat on that fool's projects.'

He walked through a dense crowd in Mary Street. Here the proletariat had gathered, at one of the mouths of their slums. They watched there, as if waiting for an opportunity to rush forth and fall upon the agents of the Government. He walked through them without seeing them. Here were the slaves of whom he had dreamt that day, as he walked through O'Connell Street, when the mystic visions were crowding in his mind and he saw an army of peasants with blood on their banners, marching on the stronghold of the slain tyrant. Now they stood, watching furtively, making no movement, in back streets; a volcano without the power of eruption. He passed through them without seeing them. They also were alien and the wild dreams of his youth were not even a memory in his mind; the vision of black hands erecting barricades.

Now he was no longer in a stupor and that word MURDERER had ceased to resound. His mind was concentrated on Tumulty and Fetch, and he felt that he had become small and cute. He would rush at them, mesmerize them and slip away to safety.

Then the feast . . . Voluptuous sights assumed dim shapes in the distance.

As he went deeper into the slums, approaching the hiding-place, his eyes began to glitter with their former ferocity and his former personality returned; but with a different aspect. His mind formed quick, pitiless decisions; but these decisions were no longer associated with ideas, unconnected with his own pleasure. The thought of pleasure, at a distance, kept recurring through devious ways, until it had rapidly assumed definite shape in his mind and he saw, as he arranged the details of his flight, a rich place, abounding with the delights of debauchery, lust and drunkenness, and his virgin body entering therein.

He did not enter the street where Tumulty had the room. Tumulty had shown them a secret entrance, through a lane at the back. He made a detour to the right and crossed a waste plot, where a house had stood and which was now used as a dumping-ground for unwanted refuse. Then he walked through a cemented path that was bound on either side by brick walls. A little door was cut into the right wall at the far end. He put his hands through a slit, like a letter-box, found a string, pulled it and opened the door. He was in the yard at the back of the house. He closed the wicket door and ran up to the back door of the house. It was ajar. He entered the house and went through deserted passages that smelt of fallen mortar. He reached the hall. On the doorstep in front, there were two old women, in shawls, talking to somebody across the street. The person, a man, was shouting something in a loud voice and the old women, one after the other, were uttering exclamations in response to what he was saying.

'It's all very well,' the man was saying, 'if (Crikey) a woman carries on like that (Janey) and robs a man of his hard-earned money . . .'

On tiptoe, without being seen or heard, McDara swiftly climbed the stairs until he passed the angle of the first flight. Then he paused and collected his thoughts, nodding his head and creasing his forehead.

'Yes, yes,' he kept saying to himself, 'that will do.'

He closed his lips tightly, drew in a deep breath and went upwards until he came to the top landing. The harlot's door was still open and there were signs on the doorstep that various feet had passed that way during the morning. There were also scraps of things on the floor and a strip of mauve cloth hanging on to the head of a nail in the door-jamb. The other inhabitants of the house had rifled the property of the taken wretch.

McDara went to Tumulty's door and knocked

four times slowly. Steps crossed the room. The door opened suddenly and he walked in. The door closed behind him immediately. The key turned.

McDara stood in the middle of the floor. Fetch was behind him at the door. Tumulty was in front, standing by the fireplace. There was no fire and the ashes of the last fire were strewn about the hearth. The room looked yellow and desolate in the spring sunlight, and it seemed, from the yellow, desolate look of the room and the musty smell, that the act had been committed there.

Neither man spoke to him in salutation. Neither did he speak. He looked closely for a moment at Tumulty's face, and seeing there an extraordinary expression, he turned to Fetch. Fetch was leaning against the door. His left eye was almost closed. His right eye was wide open. His lips grinned. His queer, twisted body was shivering slightly, giggling. He wore an expression of glee that was quite devilish; not subtly devilish, but devilish in the way that the laugh of an idiot is devilish. It was a mocking grin and it seemed to say:

'See, now. I am no longer Fetch, who once was a pimp and a hired thug. We are all equal and I am in my element. I have the laugh on you fellows.'

Then McDara turned again to Tumulty. Tumulty's face expressed a growing panic. The colour of his skin had changed. It was slightly yellow and all the hidden imperfections of his blood had suddenly shown themselves underneath the puffy skin.

The underlip was thrust out. The powerful jaws no longer denoted strength but, on the contrary, accentuated the fear in his distended eyes. His thick neck was purple. His chest heaved and his belly, that had been slightly corpulent, no longer pressed against the tip of his waistcoat. His waistcoat hung slack on his body. His legs were rigid, as if they were contemplating a revolt against his helpless body and were getting ready to dash off somewhere and destroy themselves. His hands hung down by his body with the fingers moving like the horns of a snail.

McDara examined him closely, with his hands in his pockets, screwing up his right eye. Fetch came from the door, stood beside McDara with his arms folded, nodded his head and whispered:

'Well?'

McDara looked at Fetch, with a brooding look, puckering his lips and almost closing his eyes. Then he opened his eyes wide with a sudden movement, filled his lungs and made a great effort of will, until his eyes held Fetch's eyes fixedly. Fetch unfolded his arms, licked his lower lip with his tongue, stopped grinning and then began to blink rapidly. McDara sniffed, shrugged his shoulders and said softly:

'Sit down.'

Fetch put his tongue into his left cheek, paused for a moment, raised his left shoulder and put his left hand in his pocket. McDara stared steadily at him. He pointed to a chair by the hearth. Fetch muttered something and sat down. McDara drew up another chair with his foot and sat on it. Then he looked up at Tumulty, who was still standing, with his eyes distended, his jaws stuck out and his stomach drawn up to his spine, like a yawning cat.

'Well, Frank,' said McDara, in a merry voice. 'What's the programme?'

Fetch looked up at Tumulty, opening his lips as if to say something. But he said nothing. Neither did Tumulty say anything.

'Sit down, for God's sake,' said McDara. 'Don't stand there like a stuck pig. What's the trouble? Did you get hit?'

Tumulty turned his head sideways and there was a pitiful expression in his eyes; just like an animal in pain that tosses its head and opens its slavering jaws to the sky, as if expecting that a cure from God would drop into its mouth. Then he slithered down to the floor backwards. He was unable to make any effort to hide his deplorable and shameful state. Panic had completely destroyed his self-respect.

'Let him alone,' said Fetch to McDara, in a low voice that was very fierce.

McDara did not look at Fetch and he did not appear to have heard his words.

'Well, Frank,' he continued mercilessly, 'I said I'd ask you a question afterwards, but there doesn't seem to be any need to ask it, is there? However . . . I prefer to see you in that state than making a fool of yourself in any other way. You'll be all right in the morning, unless anything else happens to you.'

Suddenly, as he uttered the last phrase, McDara turned to Fetch and stared at him fiercely. Fetch started, raised the right side of his upper lip and muttered:

'What'd happen to him?'

'What you thought was going to happen to me,' said McDara quickly, leaning close to Fetch.

Fetch started violently and the scar on his cheek, which was again uncovered, became white. His nostrils twitched rapidly and then his lips pattered, one against the other, as he muttered:

'I'm givin' ye fair warnin', not to start that bullyin' business with me. I stood for it 'slong as I had to, but now it's a different how-d'ye-do.'

Then his head began to quiver. His voice had now resumed the nasal murmur that is peculiar to the Dublin slum-dweller.

'It's no use, Gutty,' said McDara icily. 'You haven't got the courage to do me in and Frank won't stand for it. Look at him.'

He pointed at Tumulty. Fetch again raised his left shoulder and looked at Tumulty with the furtive look of a cat that is wondering whether it should bound away to safety or jump with bared claws on a hostile dog.

Tumulty thrust out his right hand towards Mc-Dara. The fingers were moving about like the horns of a snail. His face seemed to be drawn up taut to his forehead. He spoke through his clenched teeth. His voice was like that of a little boy who is boasting.

'There was no question of doin' ye in, Mac,' he said.

'That's a lie,' whispered McDara.

Suddenly Tumulty became rigid and sat up on the floor, stiffly, with his head thrust forward and his ears sticking out. He caught his hat, paused and then pulled it off his head. Holding it out in front of him, his eyes glittered and he opened his mouth.

'Stop!' hissed McDara.

Tumulty, on the verge of uttering a wild yell, remained poised with his mouth open and his hat held out in front of him. Then his arms dropped to his sides and his head fell on his chest.

He began to blubber:

'It's no damn good. I should be out now, givin' orders to my men. I'm not goin' to raise a hand against you, Mac. Ye can tell him that. But ye let us down. Ye deserted us. It's all very well for you to come in here and sneer at me. But ye believe in nothin'. I couldn't do a thing alike that. Unless a man has been a traitor and a robber of the people I couldn't touch him. If we're fightin' for freedom, our hands must be clean. There's a God above, no matter if nobody believes in Him.'

McDara looked from one to the other of them. Fetch was looking at Tumulty with hatred and contempt. McDara smiled at Fetch.

'So my guess was right, Gutty,' he said. 'Christ! You're a dangerous snake, so you are.'

The three of them sat in silence. The silence became terrifying and it seemed certain each moment, that the next moment would see them at one another's throats. But nothing happened, and as the seconds passed, the tension relaxed until their faces looked tired and bored. Tumulty sighed. His face became more normal. The panic caused by the sudden appearance of McDara was passing away. Fetch's face was still excited. He now had the worried, stupid look of a peasant who is standing with bared head in a court of law and looks from the magistrate to the prosecuting attorney and then to the jury, trying to understand what is being said and making a great effort to conceal the desire to catch up something and begin to fight and yell.

McDara's expression underwent no change. He had thought out his plan of action before he entered the room. He had the coolness of the judge and of the prosecuting attorney, who know they are protected by superior force, from the fury of the helpless peasant in the dock. And the superior force at McDara's command was intelligence, the force that is most feared by stupid people.

'Now, listen to me, boys,' he said. 'You fellows might as well throw your hat at an idea like that.'

He held out his clenched fists in front of him.

'You can't touch me,' he growled. 'And you can't do anything without me. So let up on it. There was

255

no necessity for me to come back here. I could be gone now. But I keep my word. So, let up on it. D'ye hear? I knew damn well what you'd be up to, Gutty. You don't know in the hell what to do with yourself now, so the only idea comes into your head is to have your own back, as you think. Plug everybody. Then you'd die happily. Be too much trouble to go quietly. But you'll do what I tell you all the same. Never mind, old son. Although you had it all made up to do me in, I'll forget that. There's no use grumbling because an ass brays.'

Suddenly he laughed and struck Fetch on the shoulder. Grinning, he said:

'I say, but you're a fine sort of a . . . Look here, old son, if you ever again think of doing anything, don't say a word about it to the fellow you're going to do it to. Remember the other day on the top of the tram? Eh?' He shook his head. 'I remember that all right. I remember everything. And this morning, when we were going off in the car, I remember the look in your eyes, when I jumped off and you said: "See you later." Oh! No! You don't play like that with me. Psht! You're a cod, Gutty. However! I'll forget it. Look here, old son. Shake hands. We might do a job together again. Have sense, man. Shake hands. Shake hands, I say. Don't be a fool.'

Fetch looked at McDara's outstretched hand and then at McDara's laughing eyes. His mouth was shut tight and his cheeks were sucked inwards. At last he raised his shoulders, grasped the hand and said:

'Well! I can deal with a fellah like you, but . . . that old woman . . .'

He dropped the hand, looked at Tumulty contemptuously and spat into the fireplace. Then he muttered:

'You're a washout.'

McDara looked at Fetch sombrely and said to himself:

'What sort of monster is this? Now he thinks I'm going to help him kill Tumulty, after plotting with Tumulty to kill me. Will he do what I tell him, and if so, how long will he take to plot with them for my capture?'

McDara's forehead wrinkled and he began to feel nervous at the nearness of Fetch's body. Then Tumulty spoke in a quiet, calm voice.

'Don't be so sure of yourself, Gutty,' he said, wiping his mouth with the back of his hand. There had been a little froth on his lips. 'I know now I didn't feel right about that job. That's why I fell down. But I'm not ashamed of it. I'm not a coward. Only if a man does what he doesn't believe is right, then God steps in on top of him.'

McDara's nostrils twitched. He glared at Tumulty. Fetch saw McDara's face becoming furious and his own face became expressive of a devilish glee. He bit his lower lip with his teeth and grinned.

Then Tumulty, by a sudden transformation,

seemed to recover his strength. His bare head, slightly bald over the forehead, with his ear sticking out, again looked like the head of a prize-fighter. His eyes became full of enthusiasm and they looked innocent.

'Mac,' he said. 'You have more brains than me.'

'I knew you'd begin this,' said McDara. 'All these superstitions.'

'Aye,' said Tumulty, leaning forward, with a look of religious fanaticism in his face, 'but you can't get away from it all the same. I believe and you don't, although you'd like to believe. I believe in the people. An' I'm going to go on fighting for the people.'

His head was thrown back.

'He's a washout,' snapped Fetch, eagerly watching McDara's face.

'I'll show ye whether I'm a washout or not,' cried Tumulty, jumping to his feet. 'Are ye prepared to follow me? Let's go out now and give the word. The people are in the streets. My men are ready. Come on, Gutty, if you're a man.'

Fetch opened his mouth, looked at McDara suspiciously, as if to see whether McDara believed Tumulty to be serious. Seeing a nervous expression in McDara's face, he looked at Tumulty eagerly. Then, seeing the fanatical enthusiasm in Tumulty's eyes, he jumped to his feet, standing with widespread legs. His face again assumed the expression of a cat that is wondering whether to use its bared claws in battle or its padded feet in flight.

'Are you coming, Gutty?' said Tumulty.

Fetch put his hand in his pocket and looked at McDara. A furtive, remote look of enthusiasm came into his eyes, as if borrowed from Tumulty's blazing eyes.

'What say?' he muttered to McDara. 'Will we let her rip? I don't give a damn. By the heels of the Mexican Jesus, I don't.'

Now it was McDara's turn to become panic-stricken. But his panic was different from Tumulty's. He stood up. His eyes glistened. And he began to speak with great rapidity, as if completely bereft of reason.

'Hold on,' he said. 'Wait a minute. Let me make a proposition then, if you fellows are determined to throw away your lives. Let's make a good job of it. We are no heroes now. We struck in the dark. We came like a bolt from the sky and struck and disappeared. And if we stayed hidden, as if the earth had opened up and swallowed us, the terror inspired by our hidden act would have great consequences. But if ye prefer to become heroes and undo what is done, then there is only one way to become heroes and have ballads written about you. It would be no use going out to fight, for the enemy is on the streets in force and in an hour we'd all be dead, riddled with bullets. But there is a better way and it would be a relief for me too, although I know it's cowardly and

259

it has no meaning, since we are no longer men, but living on another plane, where things have a different meaning. Let us go out together in single file and shout out to the people that we have killed him, because we believe that whenever a tyrant appears, just men must rise and sacrifice themselves to free the people from tyranny. Then we'll be taken and hanged at dawn on some fine day. They'll put the cold rope around our necks and we'll be swung off into . . . Eh? We'll die singing and people will keep singing about us for hundreds of years. Come along, then. I'll lead.'

He had spoken in a ringing voice, like the preaching of a priest, who is carried off into a fanatical state by the lure of the words he is uttering. His face shone and his legs trembled. But the effect of his words on Tumulty and Fetch was the opposite of their effect on himself. As they listened to him, the enthusiasm faded from their eyes. Their lips became contemptuous. Then they seemed to regain their normal balance by the contemplation of a mind even less sane than theirs had been just a few minutes before. They watched him until he finished, in silence. Then they looked at one another, with their mouths open; as if asking one another what to do about it. Neither saw an answer to his silent question in the other's face. So they both looked at McDara. And when they did so, they saw McDara laughing. Then they started, thinking that he had gone mad.

McDara clapped his palms together, winked at them and said, smiling sardonically:

'I told you fellows it's no use. I can always go one better than you. Listen. Do you want me to tell you more?'

Then Tumulty said in a cold tone:

'We don't want to hear any more of that stuff if that's what ye mean. I'm in earnest. This is no time for jig acting.'

McDara's eyes glittered.

'Very well, then,' he said, waving his hand towards a chair. 'Sit down and let's talk sense. Let's hear no more of this humbug. Sit down, boys.'

All three sat down. Tumulty covered his face with his hands and uttered something inaudible. Fetch sat looking towards the door, grinding his teeth and muttering. McDara sat in the middle, looking into the empty grate. His lips were open. His eyes glittered. His mind was without thought and yet he felt in a state of ecstasy, feeling the pleasant exhaustion that follows a wild flight of the imagination.

Nobody spoke for a long time. Then Fetch jumped to his feet suddenly and said:

'Blast this for a story. What are we goin' to do?'

'What's that?' said Tumulty, in a shrill, angry voice. 'Yer not askin' me, are ye? What have I got to do with it? When I put up a proposition it was turned down.'

'Who turned it down?' said Fetch. 'Think ye fellahs are goin' to use me as a toe-rag? You're a

pair o' fine mugs, you are. I'm goin' out on my own.
Hey, Mac? What about it? Where's the rest o' that
dough?'

'Ha!' said McDara, looking up, first at one, then
at the other. 'That's more like sense. Now we come
to business.'

'How d'ye mean?' said Tumulty. 'Who the hell
is going to come to business with you? I owe my
life to Ireland. I'm not goin' to throw it away like
a fool. Ye can go if ye like, but, be Christ, ye won't
get far, if ye have that in yer mind. I got ten men.'

McDara waved his hand towards Tumulty.

'Oh! Tell your ten men to go to the workhouse.
I'm fed up with you and your ten men. I was just
going to say that I owe you and Fetch some money.
That's what I came here for.'

Tumulty thrust out his lower lip and said savagely:

'I don't want your rotten money. You two are a
pair o' lousers.'

Fetch darted towards Tumulty with his hand in
his pocket.

'Easy now,' said McDara, getting to his feet.
'What's the idea, Frank?'

Tumulty, without rising from his chair, doubled
up his fists and squared himself into a fighting attitude. Looking at them fiercely, he muttered through
his teeth.

'It was all a plant,' he hissed, 'you two coming
over here, as agents-provocators. I had my fellahs
ready for something big and ye came in with yer

dirty stunt. Now ye've ruined me, but, be Christ, we're going to get even with ye. I'm no assassin in cold blood. I swore an oath to be faithful to my country and to liberate her, with arms in my hands. I'm a soldier. But ye are dirty thugs and touts, with Judas's gold in yer pockets. See me here, sitting in this chair,' he cried, striking his great chest with his clenched hands, 'a man, ready to face his fellow-men with a clean conscience. I'm no assassin. And I'll prove it too. For I'm going to publish the writ of the court martial and take the field with my men. I . . .'

He suddenly became bereft of speech and began to blubber incoherently. He stuck out his tongue. His eyes became fixed on something imaginary, which they professed to see on the wall. He put his hands to his face and crouched low. Then he gradually slithered off the chair, muttering horribly and lay on the floor, supine and motionless, still muttering.

Fetch looked at McDara. McDara felt that Fetch was looking at him. He turned slowly towards Fetch. Fetch smiled faintly. His lower lip moved. McDara started. Fetch nodded towards Tumulty. His hand moved about in the pocket of his coat, handling something bulky. Then he made a grimace, came close to McDara and said with fear in his eyes:

'He's in the jigs. He'll cough up his guts.'

'Eh?' whispered McDara.

Fetch remained silent, looking steadily into Mc-Dara's face.

'Can't ye see it?' repeated Fetch. 'He's got them all right. He's dangerous. He'll spout soon as he's questioned.'

McDara motioned Fetch away with his hand. Then he looked at Tumulty. He felt a pain in his stomach. This pain began to advance upwards towards his brain, entered his brain and he shuddered. He began to feel pity for Tumulty. Then he forgot that Fetch was present and said aloud:

'Poor Frank. Damn it! Remember that night we were up in the tree together? We were good comrades then.'

'Hey!' whispered Fetch into his ear. 'Better be quick. I tell you he'll break loose in a minute. Then I'm goin' to . . .'

'What are you going to do?' said McDara furiously, jumping to his feet.

Fetch retreated two paces, glanced with terror at the prone body of Tumulty and muttered excitedly:

'I can't stand this.'

'Come, come,' said McDara. 'Away with this damn vanity. I'm human after all. Let's all kneel down.'

He had been looking at the floor when he said this. Fetch, seeing him looking at the floor, with a queer light in his eyes, uttering extraordinary words, drew himself up and opened his mouth.

'Hey, Mac!' he whispered. 'Mac, old son!'

McDara looked up slowly. His eyes passed over Fetch's face, unseeing, and then wandered over the wall. Fetch looked over his shoulder at the wall and then turned abruptly to McDara.

Just then Tumulty moved, raised his head and said in a whisper:

'I don't feel well. I want to go to bed.'

His eyes were half closed and he was shivering.

'I'll give ye a hand, Frank,' said McDara, rushing over and putting his arm about Tumulty's shoulder. 'Come on, Gutty. Let's lift him over to the bed.'

Fetch looked on for several moments without moving. Then he began to make signs to McDara with his left hand, shaking his head at the same time.

Tumulty opened his eyes and looked at Fetch. He held out his right hand. Then Fetch ran forward, caught Tumulty's hand and began to press it.

'Hey, Frank,' he muttered. 'Ye've nothing against me, have ye? Hey, tell me.'

'Lift him,' whispered McDara gently. 'You take his legs.'

'I'll be all right,' whispered Tumulty, 'when I have a lie down. I feel dead-beat. I'm sorry, lads.'

'All right, Frank,' whispered McDara, 'we'll look after ye.'

'One of us go on each side,' said Fetch tenderly. 'Each take a leg an' an arm.'

They raised him up and staggered over to the bed with him. They put him on the bed. They put bedclothes over him. He began to breathe heavily. In a few seconds after lying down he was asleep. Fetch watched his sleeping face with his mouth wide open. McDara stared at the floor.

It was very silent in the room. Then McDara moved gently to the fireplace and sat down. Fetch followed him after a few seconds. They sat down side by side. Neither spoke. Fetch kept looking back over his shoulder at the bed, every time Tumulty emitted a loud hoarse breath through his open mouth. McDara was staring into the empty grate.

A slight wind had arisen. It rattled the window. It made a moaning sound. Afar off, beyond the closed window, there were dull sounds. In the room, it was like a tomb, with a smell of dry-rot. Time passed rapidly, while Tumulty slept and they sat waiting, as if for something to happen by the hand of fate.

Then, at last, McDara drew in a very deep breath, like a man finishing a day-dream, that has been very pleasant in a melancholy way. Without looking at Fetch, he held out his hand and caught Fetch by the arm. He pressed his arm in silence. Fetch looked suspiciously at the hand that was pressing his own and then he looked back over his shoulder at Tumulty, who was lying on his back. Tumulty's puffy cheeks were flushed and his ear stuck out. When he drew in a breath, his body swelled out and remained poised for several seconds, like a taut, oblong balloon, before he let out his breath again.

'You had better go now, Gutty,' said McDara, in a melancholy voice.

'What's that?' said Fetch, blinking.

'Listen,' said McDara.

'Eh?' said Fetch.

'You'll have to go now,' said McDara again, dreamily.

There was silence again. McDara stared into the empty grate. Fetch began to tremble. He licked his lower lip with his tongue and looked about the room. Then he got to his feet. McDara started slightly. He looked sideways slowly at Fetch. Then he smiled faintly. Fetch was looking about him, scratching his head. Then he muttered something and went on tip-toe to the bed. He got down on his stomach and crawled under the bed. He rummaged about there. Then he reappeared, dragging along the floor the parcel of food and the bottle of whisky. He came over to the fireplace on tiptoe with them. He held up the bottle and shook it. It was nearly empty. He was going to pull the cork, when McDara caught his hand.

'What about your pal?' said McDara.

Fetch looked over his shoulder at Tumulty.

'He'll need it when he wakes up,' said McDara. 'And the grub too. He'll probably have to stay here to-night. He's supposed to be down in Carlow for the week-end.'

Fetch put the parcel and the bottle on the hearth. He rubbed his palms together. Then he took his gloves from his pocket. He put them on slowly.

'Now listen, Gutty,' said McDara. 'You got to go now. Listen.'

Fetch struck his gloved hands together and spat into the grate.

'Go right away to one of Frank's men,' said Mc-Dara rapidly, 'and tell him to come along here at seven o'clock. Not before. You can find one, can't you? They are posted around here, aren't they?'

Fetch nodded his head.

'Very well. Tell one to come here at seven, not before, mind. Only one. Then you go and report for service.'

'Eh?' said Fetch, starting violently.

McDara looked him closely in the eyes.

'You had that planned out yourself, hadn't you?' he whispered.

'What? What are ye drivin' at?' said Fetch.

'Now, don't get ratty, Gutty,' said McDara quietly. 'It's a good idea. And it might be useful later on.'

'What the name o' God –' began Fetch.

'You think I don't know what passes in your mind?' said McDara, interrupting him. 'It's all right, though. I meant all along to agree with it.'

'Are you out of yer mind or what?' said Fetch excitedly. 'Frank over there like a corpse and you . . . Christ!'

'Keep quiet, man. Maybe you forgot all about it, but still and all, you had it in your mind. I know it.'

McDara looked very intently into Fetch's eyes.

'What had I in my mind?' said Fetch.

'To go back into your old crowd,' said McDara, smiling faintly.

Fetch was about to spring to his feet, when Mc-Dara touched him on the sleeve. Fetch immediately collapsed on to his chair.

'Lemme go,' he said, trembling. 'I want to clear out of here.'

'Where are you going?' said McDara, in a querulous, feminine tone.

'Eh?' said Fetch. 'I'm going to get to hell out of this town. I'm going North.'

'Why? What's the matter? Can't you listen to me?'

'No. Lemme go. This place is haunted. It's not right here. You drive me crazy. Hey. You're not above board. You got a gang. Who is supplyin' your information?'

'Now, keep quiet, Gutty,' said McDara in a tone that was very aggravating by its softness. 'Very well, of course, if you change your mind and go North, you can go. It's all right there too. I'll put them wise and they'll see that you're not interfered with. The whole situation is different now. You deserve well of the country and whatever you did before is washed off the slate. Tumulty's men, ten bloomin' men, that's no use. Why should I put my cards on the table?'

The expression of the peasant who is being brow-beaten in the dock came again into Fetch's face. As it were, he found himself cornered by McDara's guile; and even though he suspected that McDara was bluffing him, yet his stupidity was such that he was unable to prove to himself that McDara was bluffing. So he kept repeating to himself: 'He's got a secret gang. God knows who's in it. Better get out of here. Clear out of this damn country.'

'Now, keep cool, for God sake,' continued Mc-Dara calmly. 'I always keep my word and I guaran-teed that you'd make a clean getaway. So you will get away safely. Not a word. And here. . . . Take this.'

Fetch looked. McDara had another little bundle of five-pound notes in his hand, similar to the little bundle that he had handed out at the base of the Wellington Monument.

'Take this, Gutty,' he said. 'Then go. Mind, I'll keep in touch with you. I'm going away myself to make preparations for something bigger than this. This is only the beginning, Gutty. You lie low. I'll find you again and give you the nod. You might as well crawl back to New York. Or Liverpool, maybe, though New York is better. I'm going elsewhere, but there'll be something stirring shortly. Of course if ye fall down and dish out any whisper of what . . . click . . . you know. But there's no fear of that.

My idea is that if ye give a man a square deal, ye
get a square deal.'

Fetch took the bundle of notes and put them into
his pocket.

'Is that right,' he said eagerly, 'what ye said about
another job?'

'You wait,' said McDara.

Fetch held out his hand. McDara clasped it.
Then Fetch nodded towards Tumulty.

'What about him?' he muttered.

'Ye needn't worry about him,' said McDara.
'He'll be all right. I'll look after him. You send on
that fellow. Tell him to come here at seven o'clock.
Will ye be able to get out of town all right?'

'Why?' said Fetch fiercely. 'Who's goin' to stop
me?'

He laughed suddenly, pulled his gun out of his
pocket and clicked it against his hip. Then he put
it back, grinning with glee.

'I'm not afraid of anything like that,' he muttered.
'It's only when fellahs start the other sort of monkey
business. . . . I'm goin' then. Good-bye, Mac.'

A look of affection came into his eyes as he shook
McDara's hand. Then he went up to the bed on
tiptoe and looked down at Tumulty. Then he started
and walked rapidly towards the door.

'Don't forget,' said McDara. 'Tell that man to
come here at seven and then beat it.'

Fetch looked back from the door.

McDara took a pace forward, pointed the forefinger of his right hand at Fetch and said with great ferocity:

'Yes, beat it, by Jesus, or you'll die choked by a thousand devils.'

Fetch said 'God Almighty!' in a broken voice, unlocked the door and darted out, leaving the door open after him. McDara went to the door and locked it again. Then he came to the bed. He stood with folded arms, stooping forward, gazing mournfully at Tumulty's sleeping body.

And it seemed to him that with the departure of Fetch something evil had left the room. Now the room smelt fresher and it seemed to him that it was still possible to be happy. Again he felt pity for Tumulty. This feeling of pity now exalted him. Looking at Tumulty's puffy cheeks and at his skull that was beginning to grow bald, he remembered the first time he met him. He was young then, with fresh, rosy cheeks and luxuriant hair and glowing eyes. He was intoxicated with enthusiasm for an ideal life and he used to whisper on the hillside at night, when they were lying in hiding from the pursuing enemy, about a wonderful world that was going to come into being.

Now his cheeks were puffy. His hair was falling off. His stomach was swelling. His dreams had grown old in his brain. And yet he was a person to be envied, because he still dreamt. He still believed.

Looking down at the wearily breathing body, McDara was overcome with a wild desire to fondle

somebody in his arms. And he held out his hand
with a jerk, wishing to arouse Tumulty and confess
to him that he envied him.

'I am evil and you have remained innocent.'

But that was impossible. He realized with horror
that it was impossible for him henceforth to bow
down before any man, because he was proud of
knowing evil.

Despair again overwhelmed him. He dropped to
his knees by the bed, buried his face in his hands
and began to murmur:

'Mother, forgive me.'

It grew dark.

CHAPTER TWENTY-TWO

HE was aroused by hearing a church clock strike the hour. He listened, counted the strokes and learned that it was seven o'clock. He rose and took Tumulty's hand. He was about to press it fiercely, when he became afraid lest the pressure might awaken Tumulty. What should he say to him? Supposing he jumped up in the bed and cried out, accusing? Instead of pressing the hand, he held it lightly, stooped down and kissed it. Then he went to the door on tiptoe, trembling. He closed the door gently and descended the stairs. Going down the last flight, he passed a man who was going up. He caught a glimpse of the man's eyes in the dusk. He thought he had seen him somewhere before. The man went up the stairs hurriedly.

Going out the door into the street, McDara brushed against another man, who was coming in. This man caught McDara by the shoulder and growled:

'Halt! Put them up.'

McDara became transfixed with terror. He looked at the man who held him. He was a short, stout man, with a bloated face. He smelt of whisky and his voice was hoarse. He was very drunk. His fingers, clasping McDara's shoulder, moved about, as if fondling the shoulder affectionately.

'Put them up,' said the man again.

'Hush,' said McDara, leaning towards the man.

274

'Don't speak so loud. My mother is dying. I'm going for the priest.'

'Eh?' said the drunken man. 'That's a soft bar. Know who I am? Eh? Know who I am?'

'Be quick!' said McDara. 'Let me go. My mother is dying.'

'Not on your damn life,' said the drunken man. 'You come along with me. I saw ye goin' in. I followed ye. You come along. Didn't ye dart in there just now?'

'For God's sake can't you let me go?' said McDara, raising his voice. 'Who are you?'

'Who am I?' said the drunken man, in a jeering tone. 'I'll soon let ye know who I am.'

He paused, drew in a deep breath, swayed and grunted.

'I'm a detective. There ye are. Yer hash is cooked. Come 'long with me.'

At that moment, another man suddenly appeared and brushed against the drunken man, shaking him.

'Hey,' said the stranger in a gruff voice to the drunken man. 'Who the hell are you pushing against?'

'I'll give ye pushing,' said the drunken man, letting go his hold of McDara.

McDara stepped backwards. Another man was standing behind him. This man whispered in his ear:

'Get out of it quick.'

As McDara darted away, he heard somebody say in a harsh, metallic voice:

'Tumble the bastard.'

Then there was a thud, as a blow landed on the drunken man's jaw. Then there was a groan and hurried, shuffling footsteps, as they dragged the detective away somewhere.

McDara walked away, without looking back, or hurrying. For a moment only, when the man clutched his shoulder, he had felt afraid; but almost immediately his fear changed to a feeling of joy. Now the inner fears of his mind were stilled in the presence of danger. For he had to make his escape. That was the beginning. It would be more difficult at the railway station and getting on the boat. The prospect of this difficulty cheered him instead of terrifying him; because, while it lasted, there was no time for introspection.

So he walked on, musing happily, just like a man who spends his last shilling to enter a cinema, where he sits in the darkness revelling in the wild fantasies presented on the screen and enjoys them with all his senses because he knows that, in a few hours, he must go forth penniless into the streets.

He entered a little tea-shop in a side street and ordered two boiled eggs. He sat in the place after eating the meal, smoking and preparing himself for the tussle with the detectives.

At moments, while he rehearsed his replies to their questions, frightful doubts rushed into his mind, saying:

'It's madness to walk straight into their hands. They'll let nobody pass.'

And he always answered:

'Rot. 'Twill rob them of all suspicion. They'll think that no sane person would dream of walking openly out of the country after doing a job like that.'

Then he would smile in admiration of his own cleverness. It was very pleasant and he completely forgot what he had done and why he had done it. He forgot Tumulty, Fetch, his mother and the great unsolved problem of the meaning of life.

Then he got up, paid his score and walked slowly through the streets to the railway station. Now it appeared more dangerous in the streets, in the gloom and the lamplight, with the groups of detectives, soldiers and police hanging out. But again he passed unchallenged, protected from suspicion by his paltry body, his shabby clothes and his destitute eyes.

He arrived at the station booking-office just five minutes before the boat train was timed to leave. He took his place in the queue before the window of the booking-office and then looked casually across the room towards the door that led on to the platform. A ticket-checker was standing there as usual, but there were two men standing beside the ticket-checker. They had their hands in their pockets and they examined every one that passed. As McDara reached the window, they halted a young man who had just presented his ticket to the checker. McDara's breath caught in his throat.

'Liverpool, third single,' he said in a firm voice.

He got his ticket, put his change in his pocket and turned towards the door, where the two men were standing beside the ticket-checker. They had allowed the young man to proceed. McDara handed his ticket to the checker. The checker punched it. McDara could not resist glancing furtively at one of the detectives. That glance probably aroused their suspicions, for they both stepped in front of him when he tried to pass.

He opened his mouth and looked up at them. His toes itched.

'Where are ye goin'?' said the man on his right, gruffly.

'Liverpool,' said McDara.

'Who are ye?'

'What's yer name?'

'Where d'ye come from?'

'What are ye goin' to Liverpool for?'

They asked him half a dozen questions before he could answer. He tried to answer but his tongue clung to the roof of his mouth and he could only stammer.

'Eh?' said one of the detectives to the other. 'What about this?'

A white-haired lady, with very thin legs, called out in a shrill voice:

'Allow me to pass, please.'

They took no notice of her. The lady's voice, for some reason or other, restored McDara's self-control.

'My name is Carter,' he said in an angry voice. 'I belong to Liverpool. I'm going over to look for a ship. I came over here because I was out of work and I had a friend, Miss Todd of Blackrock. I was batman to her brother in France. I'm an ex-soldier, discharged for shell-shock. She gave me a letter to Colonel Johnson and . . .'

Here the white-haired lady, with very thin legs, called out in a shrill voice:

'Of course you would persecute a poor ex-service man. Shell-shock too. Dear me! Will I ever get out of this country before I'm murdered in my bed? What rudeness! Let me pass, please. Not another night. . . . Poor man! I do hope you get a job. And never come back here again. You'll be murdered in your bed, poor boy. It's . . . it's shocking!'

'Now, ma'am . . .' began one of the detectives.

'I have my papers,' said McDara to the other detective. 'D'ye want to see them, and here's a telegram from Colonel Johnson, telling me to report. . . .'

'Get out of it,' hissed the detective at McDara, giving him a push on to the platform. 'We're only doin' our duty, ma'am.'

'It's scandalous!' said the white-haired lady, walking with great dignity on to the platform. 'You're even more rude than the French.'

And she bustled up to the train, followed by a

porter, who was staggering under a load of suitcases and trunks, that were covered with all sorts of labels.

McDara entered a third-class carriage. The train moved off. There was a cold sweat on his forehead and he could not keep his legs from trembling. There was only one other person in the carriage, a young woman who was reading a periodical and giggling. McDara kept putting his hand furtively to his trembling knees and holding them; but when he took away his hand they started trembling again. The giggling of the young woman irritated him fearfully and he wanted to say to her angrily:

'How can you giggle like that when the country is in mourning for a horrible crime!'

Then his knees suddenly stopped trembling. He looked at the young woman with contempt and began to repeat in a strange manner to himself mechanically that Ireland was a country where one might be murdered in one's bed, that he would never spend another night in it and that the detectives were more rude than the French.

The train arrived at the pier. He walked hurriedly across the wooden planks to the gangway. He was not halted there, and as he walked up the gangway, into the steerage quarters, he suspected that this was a trap and that they would catch him on board. He went down the ladder into the cabin. He sat down, looked at the deck and waited. Nothing happened. Nobody came near him. The ship's engine

began to turn. The ship moved off. His lips began
to tremble.

'Christ!' he kept saying to himself. 'Am I away?
Have I pulled it off?'

The cabin was now crowded. Everybody was
talking. Sailors and stewards were rushing about.
Women were trying to find a place to lie down.
Three migratory labourers, smoking clay pipes, stood
near the bar, waiting for it to open. A stout man,
with large flat feet, had come aboard drunk and was
standing on the middle of the deck, searching in his
pockets and calling everybody that passed, to tell
them some long rambling story. There was an end-
less turmoil and this was increased when the deck
began to quiver and the machinery of the ship began
to rattle, as if everything had suddenly broken loose
and screws, iron bolts and the hinges of doors were
drifting about, banging against everything that
came in their way.

The noise was not really very loud, but to
McDara's ears it was as loud as thunder; even the
patter of the waves against the ship's sides was
amazingly loud. The noise, a tumult without purpose, made him feel that he had really escaped, that
there was no further danger, that everybody had
escaped, including the screws, bolts, hinges, the
deck and the man with the flat feet, who was searching in his pockets and muttering to himself. The
sea, pattering against the ship's sides, was pushing
them all away from a damned place, where the cry

of MURDERER was in the air. Now everything was lost and forgotten and never again need his heart grow cold with fear or remorse.

Through the port-holes came the salt smell of the sea and the cold of night coming over waves. He felt a desire to have a last look at the land from which he was flying. He got up from his seat and went on deck. He leaned over the side. A girl was standing beside him, with a handkerchief to her eyes, looking hungrily towards the land. Although it was dark and the shore was already growing dim in the distance, she kept waving her free hand and whispering good-bye, either to the motherland or to some dear one she had left behind.

McDara, hearing her sob, looked at her. Then he looked towards the land. He saw the dim, upheaving shore, the mountain peaks, the swaying lights and the sky overhead, clouded with the shadows of night. Wild grief came upon him in a flash. He bowed his head and laid his cheek against the iron wall of the ship. He felt that something was being torn out of him by the vanishing shore and by the mountains that seemed to be raising themselves on tiptoe to catch a last glimpse of him. He remembered with terrible clearness every beautiful thing he had ever seen in Ireland, every kind word, every joyful moment. And these memories formed themselves into a picture of Heaven from which he was being cast out.

'An outcast!' he muttered to himself. 'Now I have

lost everything. Henceforth I am a wanderer on the face of the earth.'

In the night, the wallowing ship became a monster, pouring fire and smoke from its bowels, cutting the black back of the sea with its pointed head, while in its wake, swirling white waves fell row on row into the darkness.

Sea spray washed the ship's side and fell upon his pale face with a hissing sound.

He sank into a stupor. Now nothing mattered, and if anybody questioned him, he would wearily admit that he was the assassin. It was no longer pleasant to live. He stayed there, with his cheek laid against the cold iron until the ship reached Holyhead.

As he was walking ashore along the gangway, he paused and said to himself:

'Where am I going? Why go any farther?'

Somebody pushed him from behind and said:

'Move on, mate.'

He entered the train, sat in the corner of a carriage, dropped his head on his chest and began to doze. He fell asleep, utterly exhausted. He began to dream when the train moved.

His dream was not a succession of visions but a single vision, sustained through what seemed to him to be an eternity of time. It was a vision of the scene where the assassination had been committed. Every detail stood out even more clearly than in reality. He could smell the sap of the budding trees

283

and see the particles of mica gleaming in the gravel that was strewn on the road. He could feel the warmth of the wooden seat where he had sat. The sun had shone on it. He could also feel the moist warmth of the sun, full of the flavours that had been sucked up from the germinating earth. He could see Fetch's lips and his cruel eyes. He could see the red tabs on Tumulty's stockings. He could see HIS face. It kept bobbing back and forth and there was a look of wonder in the eyes. Why? Why?

Then again the smell of the rich earth came into his nostrils and a tramp, wearing the white smock of a medical student, halted in front of him and saluted him with upraised stick, saying:

'Give it to the bastard!'

It was always noon in this vision; just like a summer noon, when time ceases to exist and nothing moves but the jaws and the wagging ears of prostrate sheep, through all eternity.

He was awakened suddenly and found an official standing over him asking for his ticket. He looked around him stupidly. The carriage was crowded with people. They were all laughing at him. They thought he was drunk. He fumbled in his pockets and found the ticket.

'Change at Chester for Liverpool.'

McDara opened his mouth stupidly and said:

'Eh? But I'm going to London.'

The people laughed again, thinking he was drunk.

'Well! Ye better get another ticket at Chester, then. Don't forget now.'

McDara looked at the people with weary eyes and buried his face in his hands. The official left the carriage. Somebody said to McDara:

'Have another sleep. I'll wake ye up when we reach Chester.'

'Eh?' said McDara stupidly, raising his head.

The people laughed again, thinking he was drunk. Then he grew angry with them and said with great ferocity:

'Christ died for us all, didn't he?'

The people stopped laughing and looked at him with interest. Then he became afraid that he had acted suspiciously. With that, he recovered control of himself and remembered everything; that he was making his escape, that he must get another ticket at Chester and that he must get to London and meet Kitty Mellett before he killed himself.

This was an extraordinary revelation to his mind, that he was going to London to meet Kitty Mellett and that he was going to kill himself afterwards. And he became so stupefied at the knowledge that this dual purpose had existed in his mind without his being aware of it, that he again opened his mouth and swayed about on his seat, like a drunken man.

'Let him alone,' he heard somebody say. 'The best of us take a drop over the mark now and again.'

He got up and went into the corridor. He stood there until the train reached Chester. He went out to the booking-office and bought a ticket for London. He returned to the train and entered another carriage that was almost empty. Without looking at the two men who were sitting there, he sat down, leaned his head against the cushion and closed his eyes. The train moved off. He thought:

'That is extraordinary. There is no use struggling then if I can't kill my conscience. Is there a God, then? Some unknown Being, of whom I never dreamt?'

He fell asleep again. Again the vision returned, distinct with the wooden seat, the heap of gravel and the grey orchard wall.

Once more he was roused by an official and asked for his ticket. He had the ticket clutched in his hand and he gave it up. The man said:

'London next stop.'

McDara sighed and sat up. He heard the rushing sound of the train and through the window he could see lights flashing past in the darkness.

Holy Cross Cottages; Holy Cross Tipperary -
$375 a week -